TAKE A SEAT AT THE
COSMIC CAMPFIRE

DHARA PAREKH

For my sisters, Megha and Vaidehi,
The permanent seat-holders at my campfire. One brought sustenance and a zest for life; the other, hot tea and a quiet understanding.

And to my honorary sister, Dharati, who joined in with skits and French pastries.

CONTENTS

INTRO

It's the heart of winter. You find yourself wandering alone in a dense thicket. The tips of your fingers are frosted, and your nose could extinguish a match with a sizzle. A bitter chill bites at your skin, and your breath billows like ghostly tendrils in the air. Your body is frigid, and so is the world, and you crave more than just physical warmth—you long for a hearth to ignite your mind and soothe your soul.

So I call out to you to propose a remedy—stories. Around a campfire. On a cliff, beyond that forest, under a moonless sky so dark it mirrors the resplendent Milky Way.

Following my voice, you arrive at the cliff. I invite you to take a seat at the campfire. The fire first roars like molten lava, gently toasting your brumal skin, and then settles into a symphonic crackle. It reminds you of the Big Bang—an explosion and then a cosmogonal choreography. You settle on a comfortable log, but you are not alone.

Around the fire, a congregation of interstellar travelers, much like yourself, huddles closely, swathed in cozy blankets. I pass around hot beverages. You choose your preferred one, cradling the cup in your freezing hands. The warmth of a thousand sunrises pulsates through your skin, providing respite from the relentless cold.

The newfound stillness gives you a chance to hear the faint whispers of distant galaxies. Curious, you look above at the constellated sky—each star a distant sun, each one a storyteller in its own right.

The ashy surface of the burnt wood splits like a weathered map of red fiery cracks. "Don't they look like pathways to undiscovered realms?" I ask.

You peer through the fire for an answer. It flickers, casting an orange glow on your face. You swear you saw a swirling nebula in it. Something grazes your cheek, but you can't determine if it's a spark from the fire or stardust from the nebula within.

Of course, the fire harbors mysteries. It's the guardian of ancient tales, after all, preserving them through generations. It shelters narratives ignited by wanderers like you. Together, we visualize a memory of the first story ever told around the first fire among the first group of celestial explorers. In this moment, you realize that you are part of something greater than yourself—a storytelling tradition that transcends time and space.

We brace ourselves, yet gravity seems to release its hold on us. The blazing campfire becomes our sun, and we, like planets, gravitate toward it. Our yearning for stories revolves around us like moons.

An electrifying anticipation fills the air as the wood crackles and pops, as if it, too, longs to divulge its secrets. An ember ascends and joins a constellation overhead. In return, a meteor streaks from the sky, rekindling our fire.

Now I, a fellow traveler, am ready with a gunny full of stories slung over my shoulder. Stories inspired by the whispers of the galaxies, stories that explore our condition when confronted with sudden change. These are stories born from my own fascination with the unknown, the uncharted, and the unfathomable.

In the first story, you will step into the realm of time travel.

The second will thrust you on a space opera quest alongside a father and daughter.

The third story will pull you into a dark dystopia of Augmented Reality.

In the fourth, you will venture into the rocky terrain of Planet Tul and its colonization.

Our cosmic campfire will conclude with a steampunk adventure through the marvels of the solar system.

It's time. We are about to bend time and space, experience raw human grief, meet a spaceship commander like never before, listen to the arguments of sentient spaceships, savor Ice Golas on Europa, and fight space pirates. So, pull those blankets closer and take one more sip.

On this cliff, where the boundaries of reality blur and the universe becomes our playground, we will voyage together to the farthest reaches of the cosmos and traverse the wonders of science fiction. Let this campfire serve as our anchor.

The firewood is crackling with astronomical energy, the flames are rippling across the fabric of spacetime, the mugs are radiating interstellar warmth, and the boundless galactic mysteries gleam from above. Why, even the logs themselves seem to hum with secrets of the universe. So, take a seat again.

The cosmic campfire awaits.

1. ALLONS-Y!

Megha flung her laptop and launched off her bed when she saw an old woman materialize in the middle of her bedroom. The woman was in her sixties, plump and tired, with her torso curved like a saucer and her arms slumped from the sockets.

"Who…who are…" Fear sent Megha's heart into a rapid drumbeat. She glanced at the bedroom door, ready to run, but the woman, who looked a lot like her mother, was blocking the entrance. "How did you…"

The old woman gazed at the small room, agape. Her teary eyes danced.

"Oh, the memories," she mumbled.

Megha wondered if she had dozed for a while, and her mummy[1], who was out of town with her pappa for a Mundan[2] ceremony, had put on scary make-up and decided to make her daughter shit her pants.

She looked at her laptop and then back at the woman. Definitely not asleep. This wasn't a dream either because the cut she got this morning stung her hand.

"Who are you?" Megha pushed herself into a corner. "How did you get inside? I'll…I'll call the police."

Spirits and ghosts had never frightened her; she thought them a laughable concept, a manifestation of oppressed minds or vivid imaginations. But at this moment, she wished this person were a haunting spirit seeking salvation and not a serial killer out to collect a chunk of her hair as a trophy. She didn't want to die at the ripe age of twenty-one.

"Put that phone aside," the woman spoke. Her mouth was a well, rimmed with age; her face as dark as a cave. "I am not going to hurt you." The papery skin on her neck undulated as she talked.

There had been no smell in the room before. Maybe there had been—of the tempering of asafoetida from the dinner

---

[1] Many Indian adults, particularly Gujaratis, use "Mummy" to address their mothers, challenging the Western association of the term with childhood

[2] An act of shaving a baby's birth hair which is celebrated ceremoniously in certain cultures of India.

her mother had cooked that evening, of the wetness of the monsoon, and of the sandalwood incense from the neighbor's—but Megha was accustomed to them. Now that the old woman had spoken, her breath had taken over the air, leaving a whiff of metal and tobacco across the room.

Megha raised her voice and phone-laden hand. "Who are you?"

"I will tell you if you calm down."

There was something about the woman's face. She was not her mother, but she bore a familiarity that made Megha feel safe, as if she was with someone she knew. She lowered her arm and sat at the corner of her bed.

The stranger sat at the opposite corner with her legs crossed under her. Only the light of the table lamp illuminated their faces in the 1:00 AM darkness of Mumbai.

"Look…" the old woman coughed, then placed her arms on her thighs and spoke again, "I only have an hour, so you have to start believing things fast and ask fewer questions, okay?"

"Who. Are. You?"

"I will answer that. Just tell me this first. When are you leaving for the US?" She peeked at the large world map hung on the wall above the bed.

"How do you…?"

"Just tell me, and I will answer all the questions. I promise."

Megha shifted a bit and clutched the carrom[3] board propped against the adjacent wall—something to block the old woman if she attacks. Next to it, she located the box of boric acid powder[4], always kept in tandem with the board. Something to throw at the woman's face to buy some time. Once content with her weapons of choice, she responded.

"January. In six months."

"Okay…okay. We have time."

"Time for what?"

The old woman looked at Megha and spoke in a calm, breathy voice.

"I am you. From the future."

"Oh, come on!" As ridiculous as it sounded, Megha couldn't help but lean forward and observe the woman's face. She did look like an older version of herself. Same beady eyes that were a mix of curiosity and mischief but bagged with puffiness. Same thick, wavy hair, but gray, frayed, and tied in a bun, unlike her usual ponytail. Same rounded lips but creased. Same height but curved at spine.

---

[3] A tabletop game of Indian origin
[4] A fine-grained powder commonly used on the carrom board to enable the pieces to slide more easily

"See, I have been you," the woman said, "so I know that even if a part of you believed me, you wouldn't admit it and would keep questioning and ridiculing me. So, how about this? I will tell you things that prove I am you, and then you shut up and listen?"

Megha stayed quiet. She glanced at her window. It was dark and quiet outside. Only the gentle patter of the rain and the whooshing sound of occasional trucks blazing down the Western Express Highway, leaving trails of light on the damp buildings. She rubbed her cheeks. Definitely awake. Was someone playing a prank on her? Must be that Akshay from the second floor. He had been salty ever since he lost to her at carrom.

But that wasn't possible. She looked at the doors of her bedroom and balcony. They were both shut. There was no way this person entered through a door. She had seen it with her own eyes. The woman had appeared out of nowhere.

Megha sat straight and nodded in agreement. If something went wrong and her carrom-attack wouldn't suffice, she would lunge for the balcony door, grab the motorbike helmet hanging from its hook, and hurl it at the woman's face. She'd then run into the balcony and scream bloody murder from their four-story apartment.

"Okay. Good," the old woman said. The stench of tobacco permeated the room again, weaving through the scattered clothes, towels, and tools before dissipating in a corner with a glass shelf displaying dusty, handcrafted wicker figurines that didn't appear to be arranged by the room's occupant.

"Don't spew random facts," Megha dictated. "Tell me things only I would know."

"Wait. What's for dinner tonight?"

"Why?"

"Just tell me."

"Dal, bhaat, rotli…some shaak[5], I think."

"You think?" The woman twisted her head.

"I haven't checked. My mother made it before she left."

"Then, what did you eat?"

"Instant noodles."

"Featherbrain jad hu[6]!" the old woman cursed multilingually and spat. Fibers of tobacco sprayed from between her gums and inner cheek. "Bring me a plate of that dinner."

Megha wanted to deny it, but she reminded herself this person might be her. She didn't want to deprive herself of food. Plus, it was a good way to check if this woman would let her leave the room.

---

[5] A meal of dal (lentil soup), bhaat (rice), shaak (cooked and spiced vegetables), and rotli (wheat flatbread) constitutes the staple diet of most Gujaratis
[6] Pig-headed, stubborn

She did.

Megha went to the kitchen, grabbed a knife, and hid it in one of her cargo pants' numerous pockets.

Then, she filled a thali[7] full of food and a big glass of sugarcane juice, her favorite.

The woman was still seated at the edge of the bed, thinking something.

"Here." Megha handed her the plate and glass and then turned on the tubelights. Swinging from one corner of the room to another was a rope with rain-soaked clothes flopping from it. She bent and navigated beneath the limp clothes to her side of the room, her mother's damp petticoat[8] brushing against her nape.

"I was wondering if I should go outside and look at our house," the woman voiced her thoughts. "See Mummy Pappa's room. I miss them so much. But I don't want to risk it. It might set something off. I was only supposed to come to this spot."

"O…kay," responded Megha, her eyes partially closing in ridicule

"Oh, goodness! These steel thalis. I totally forgot!" the woman squealed and cradled the heavy plate.

---

[7] A plate made of metals. A 'Thali' sometimes also refers to an Indian-style meal made up of a selection of various dishes which are served on a platter.
[8] An innerwear/underskirt worn under a saree

Megha's round face turned into a donut of wrinkles. Who jumps at the sight of a plate? She thought.

"What's this?" The woman peered into the glass.

"I got some sugarcane juice this evening."

"I haven't had it for decades!" she shrieked, wide-eyed, and took a sip of the chilled, sweet nectar.

"Ah…memories. Such powerful memories. School summer vacations," she shared. "Loitering around in the hot sun on a bike and stopping at that stall at the end of our street. Remember that funny uncle in greasy banyan[9]? He would shove sugarcanes in the mill and pretend his hand went with it. That always freaked me out." She took another sip. "I can still hear the jingling of the bells he had hung on the green wheel that he churned."

Megha remembered it well. She still saw the funny uncle every now and then. Only, he wasn't funny anymore because he had lost his business and wiped tables at a Dosa[10] place now. She remembered how, as a kid, she would wait for the guy's mangled hand to appear on the other side of the mill along with pulped canes, but only the juice of sugarcanes would fill the bowl underneath it.

----

[9] Vest or undershirt
[10] A savory crepe. By adding "place" next to the word, it is used here to refer to a south-Indian restaurant

The old woman emptied the glass and flashed a big, teary smile.

With one hand, Megha gripped the large earthen flower vase, her other hand ready with the phone, just in case her other attacks don't do enough damage.

She watched as the woman mixed everything on the plate—fragrant grains of local rice, sweet and tangy lentil dal, stir-fried potatoes and cabbage tossed in mustard seeds and spices, and the shredded mango pickle—and took hearty, monstrous bites, one after the other. She kept her gaze fixed as the old woman guzzled until there was nothing left.

"Some more, please." The woman lifted the thali.

Megha refilled it out of pity.

This time, the old woman was crafty, a keen concentration on her face. She placed a spoonful of potatoes and cabbage on rotli—a thin, soft flatbread made from whole wheat—dipped them into the dal, and popped it in her mouth as she see-sawed her shoulders.

The sight stirred memories for Megha, harking back to her childhood when she used to perch on the kitchen countertop to sip the piping-hot broth that her mother used to skim off the boiled split pigeon peas before blending them for the dal.

"Ahhh…" The old woman ate another bite.

Megha cringed, repulsed by the woman's moaning. She reached up, shoving her mother's saree on the clothesline to the side so she could look the woman in the eye. "Enough…you. Answer my questions," she demanded.

"If it seems too odd for you to call me by your name, you can call me Meg."

"Meg?" Megha crinkled her nose again.

"Yes. You renamed yourself after living a couple of years in the US because they kept calling you Mega. You'll learn the rhotic pronunciation of 'R,' but they won't be able to pronounce our consonants."

"I'll note that down," Megha spoke in a flat tone. "Now, why should I believe you are me?"

"Oh yes." The old woman blanketed half the rotli, clutched dal-soaked bhaat under it, and shoved it in her mouth. "Righth befoh I appeayead…" She swallowed and smacked her lips. "You were flexing your bloated biceps and smiling at them."

Megha broke eye contact and looked sideways, rubbing her arms.

"You could have been snooping before you dropped in," she argued.

"You make fun of people for using those sites, but an hour ago, you were pinning different places of North America to your Wanderlust board."

"A thirteen-year-old hacker could tell me that."

The old woman frowned at Megha and got back to eating.

When she finished all the food on her plate, she walked to the washbasin just outside the room and, with her one foot still inside, washed her hands.

Megha watched as she came back, walking like an old lady. A strange empathy formed within her. As if the sight of watching an old person eat like that wasn't sad enough.

"Let's see." The woman wiped her hands on her pants, sat on the bed, and began, "You secretly ate during all the religious fasts Mummy made you keep. No one knows that. It was you who stole that girl's bike for a day when you were in eighth grade. You boasted about it to your friends when you were older but you didn't tell them you wrote a 'sorry' letter to the bike girl. You haven't kissed anyone yet, but you did help someone lose their virginity on this very bed."

Megha's mouth opened.

"Bastard, this humidity. One thing I don't miss." Old Megha coughed into the sticky air and then continued.

"You cheated on your board exams. You built your first machine when you were twelve, an electric Styrofoam cutter, because you were tired of cutting them for school projects. You pride yourself on the fact that you don't like small talk, but girl, *no one* likes small talk. You are not special. You don't like sitting inside a restaurant. It seems claustrophobic. You change the layout of your room when you have nothing going on in your life because it gives you an illusion that life isn't stagnant. Now that you didn't know, did you? I figured it out. It's because we hate when things stay the same."

The woman studied the room. There were marks and scratches all over the walls from frequent furniture rearrangements. With no response from Megha, she carried on.

"When asked to follow rules, you experience a sensation akin to being tied with a rope and submerged underwater. You project strength, but a peculiar heat churns in your stomach when something ill happens to Mummy or Pappa. You say fame doesn't excite you, but secretly, you want to do something great for which you are remembered forever. You have never been in love. You have never been drenched in rain, despite living in this city. You drink lukewarm black chai. Never had a steamy hot meal. That's what bothers me the most. Never feeling the need to pounce on a lip-smacking, steaming-hot meal."

Old Megha let out a tired breath and rubbed the small of her back.

"This godforsaken spine," she mumbled to herself and stretched out on the bed. "Ahhh…" She unclogged her molars with her fingernail, crossed one foot over her knee, and rested her hands beneath her head. The woman gazed at Megha once more and remarked, "And your one true obsession is to replace the robots. What does that even mean?"

Megha absorbed it all, shocked and vulnerable. If this was indeed her future self, and she disappeared, regret would haunt her forever. The senile woman had been dead on about one more thing. Although she now believed the woman, her basic instinct was to ridicule and discredit her.

Megha glanced back at her future self. Not once had she ever imagined what she might be like as an elderly individual. The visual before her was not pretty. However, unlike her, her older self exuded an unwavering lack of inhibition and a surreal sense of comfort in her own skin.

Megha liked it.

"Where are you in the future right now?" she asked. "How did you manage to come here…to the past?"

"Exactly a week ago, I found a clock outside my door. You know those clocks you used to see pictures of…from the Victorian era?

"Steampunk?" Megha's eyes grow wide.

"Hoarder of useless trivia, aren't you?" Old Megha chuckled. "Yes, it was like that. A heavy, jagged, gunmetal clock with a big, brown dial. It had metal cogs and gears around the dial that spun as the hands ticked. Not just that. It also had a compass, an earth globe—quite faded, and a mechanical GPS of some sort that displayed my coordinates at that moment. The compass's needle, the point on the globe, they were all in working condition, but somehow, they remained fixed. The only thing I could manipulate were the coordinates.

"I joked around with it for a week, inputting the coordinates of random cities. Nothing happened. A part of me knew it wasn't an ordinary clock. Its parts didn't move like a machine. They were…lifelike, like how our eyes blink and our limbs move. I decided what I'd do if I could travel to the past, even though it felt absurd. Then, today, I tried the coordinates of this location. Something clicked, and boom! I was here."

"Wow."

"Yes. Oh, and behind the clock was a timer. And a note. It read, 'Allons-y.' The universe never stops surprising us, does it?"

Megha locked eyes with her older self. A sweaty, sticky, lifeless face stared back at her.

"What has happened…in the future?" she asked, attempting to imagine the cruel events that might have led her future self to this state. "Has the world gone wrong? Is it dystopian?"

Old Megha laughed.

"Listen to you talk. Like a robot. Dystopian," she mocked the last word, imitating Megha.

"Tell me."

"The future." The old woman took a deep breath. "No, it's not dystopian. The world where I come from is as good as it's going to get. Comfortable housing for all, health care, education, equality, democracy. Even the shins don't get bruised anymore."

"Then why do you look so miserable?" Megha asked. "If it's perfect, why are you visiting the past as if to ask for help?"

"Because something happened before this world got better. First, there was a war. Then, the world boycotted the USA. We became an independent planet of sorts with no connection to other countries. The people there aren't allowed to go out, and no one and nothing from the outside is allowed in. We cannot go to India or meet our family. Everything from our life outside the US disappeared. Poof." Old Megha snapped her fingers and placed her hand under her head again. "Then came the revolution. But it was too late. The world didn't want us anymore. No one was surprised. I…we lived a crazy life. We appreciate the independence and freedom, yet there is loneliness. Haunting loneliness. As if we are living in a vacuum. Nothing comforts us anymore." Her eyes welled up.

"I am sorry," said Megha, her chest warming up. She had never imagined experiencing loneliness, always finding solace without the need for others. It made her wonder if her older self defined loneliness the same way she did—the feeling that stems from the absence of people. "What can I do?" she asked.

Old Megha sat up.

"Before you move to the US, I want you to learn to cook Mummy's dal bhaat. All Indian food, actually."

Megha stared at her future self in disbelief.

"What kind of medieval times have you come from?" She sneered.

"I am from the future."

"Then why are you making such a patriarchal request?"

"There is nothing patriarchal about being self-reliant or having the ability to feed yourself. Don't let that stop you from living your best life."

Megha stood and walked back and forth in the tiny space between her bed and her desk.

"How old are you now?" she said. "I forgot to ask."

"Sixty-six."

The answer stunned Megha. To her, the woman looked older than eighty.

"Okay, so let me get this straight." Megha ground her teeth. "I live forty-five long years in a foreign country, suffering loneliness, wars, losses, and a revolution. Then I come across a freakin' time machine, and instead of using it in the countless, wicked ways that I am already picturing in my head right now, I come to this mundane moment in our life with that request? I should have traveled to that one time when I entered my email password incorrectly and stop that from happening."

"You should lose that sarcasm." Old Megha folded her hands. "It's not going to take us far in life."

"I can see that," Megha stated as she looked at her from the corner of her eye. Her older self did seem like her. She was wearing loose pants and a tight olive green tank top that braced the bulge around her waist. Megha glanced at her own clothes, a similar tank top over toned abs and cargo pants. They were alike. Then why was her future self being unbelievingly stupid?

"I just can't wrap my mind around it," Megha added. "You could go anywhere, do anything, or see the world. You could have seen our parents!"

"You may not grasp it now because you are a young girl, sitting in the comfort of your childhood home, aware that everything you need is within arm's reach. You will come to understand when you are living alone in a foreign land at sixty-six, discerning the difference between what's truly essential and what's merely fascinating, the difference between need and want, and the discipline to prioritize the former."

"It's not that big of a deal. Mummy and Pappa moved to this city when they were young, too, to a different culture and state. Yet they fared well. I'll be okay, too."

"No, they didn't fare well, you fool! And you aren't moving to a different state. You are moving across the globe!"

"Yes, although…"

"Listen. I can't tell you much, but a lot will come in our life and more will walk away," said Old Megha. Her tight jaw softened, relaxing her lips. "In all that chaos, you'll need something to anchor yourself, something that comforts you, reminds you of who you are. People die. Food is a constant. I can travel to the past to see Mummy and Pappa or visit that giant saw in Tokyo that we've always wanted to see, but what would one hour of that get me? What I am asking right now will impact the quality of our entire life."

"But why cooking? You must have forgotten how much we hate it. It's too…traditional."

"Because the only way to ensure that you can enjoy the food you love for the rest of your life is by learning to cook it yourself. It's about creating a sense of familiarity in a world that can be frightening and unfamiliar. In a world plagued by wars and destruction, Mummy's dal bhaat will preserve your sanity and health. It might sound ridiculous, but trust me."

Megha squinted her eyes at Old Megha.

"When did we become so domestic?"

The old woman laughed through fits of cough and tapped her knee. It improved Megha's mood, too. Her own laughter.

"Fine, okay. I don't get it, but let's accept that food impacts us so much," Megha said. "But won't I be able to just get it from a restaurant?"

"No one makes it the proper way, let alone prepare it like Mummy does. Over the years, Indian food has deviated so far from its authentic version. It's as different as, say, Gujarati is from Python."

"There's a Python cuisine?"

"Talking about languages, you featherbrain."

"Well, then, can't you travel to the point in history where everything started to change and prevent it from happening or something?"

"It doesn't work that way. People didn't wake up one day to find that everything they enjoyed about their food had vanished," the old woman explained. "You don't eat Pav Bhaji[11] one day and then discover it's gone from the

---

[11] "Bhaji" refers to a spiced mixture of mashed vegetables served with pav, a soft bread roll. This street food dish has its origins in Mumbai, India.

restaurant's menu the next morning. No. It's a gradual process, the erasure. First, Pav Bhaji turns into a mild vegetable dish with dinner rolls. Then it takes the form of a mushy stir-fry, and before you realize it, the colors and spices disappear, and you are eating mashed potatoes with sliced bread."

"Okay, okay. But isn't that inevitable, the food transformation? We don't eat what our great-grandparents ate." Megha shrugged and then paced back and forth. "Hey, how about I compile all these recipes into a book or something?"

"Twenty years from now, you won't have anything you have right now, not even your email. The world changes fast, really fast. Nothing lasts but memories and skills. Besides, merely jotting down a recipe is not enough if you don't comprehend the process."

Megha sighed and sat on the bed. She thought and thought as Old Megha waited for her younger self to be convinced.

"Wait…" the twenty-one-year-old spoke, looking at the ceiling. "You have…I mean, *we* have already lived this life. How can I change what has already happened? And if I can change, shouldn't I just return to India before the border closes? Or just don't go there? No, no. I do want to go. How about I stop all of this from occurring? Somehow reach the top and prevent the US from becoming the political outcast? Huh?"

"One must have never felt the need to punch their own self so hard before," Old Megha mumbled as she glared at Megha.

"What?"

"I don't know much, but there are rules. I am sure I can only change aspects of our life. Even our own events that might influence other big events will cancel out. The clock won't let me travel there."

"Right, right. Because of the butterfly effect," said Megha. "I saw it in a movie."

Old Megha clasped her hands and exercised restraint.

"This little change might be important to us," she said. "But in the grand scheme of things, learning cooking skills is so insignificant that these rules won't affect it. Even if it doesn't work, what do we have to lose, huh?"

When Megha didn't reply, the old woman stood and began to pace back and forth on the other side of the bed, nearly tripping over the dumbbells strewn across the floor.

"The big events that happened are permanent. Fixed points," she explained. "No one can change them, I am sure. But little things that you and I alter are not going to matter."

"But wouldn't the actions of smaller individuals lead to those big events?"

"Yes, but if their actions have led to bigger events, then they are not small individuals. They have already become important, bigger individuals in this matrix," Old Megha clarified.

"Okay…okay. I got it."

"Look, you keep forgetting that whatever thought crosses your mind has already crossed mine. We are the same person. The only difference is I am forty-five years older, hence wiser. So trust me when I say that an unimportant girl from India learning to cook in her twenties so she can self-sufficiently feed herself healthy, scrumptious food in the future is not going to impact bigger events."

"Then…" Megha sat down and threw her hands in the air. "What's the purpose of all this?"

"What do you mean?"

"This whole life, my existence. If I am so insignificant in the grand scheme of things," replied Megha, her shoulders mirroring the posture of her future self.

Old Megha walked toward the other side of the bed and sat next to her.

"I wish I had an answer for that."

They sat in silence for a while.

"Why didn't you bring the clock with you?" asked Megha. "You could have left it with me. I would have used it our whole life to travel to India and eat whatever we wanted."

"I couldn't bring the clock with me or even other objects. Just me in my clothes. And this!" The woman pushed her tongue out. A slobbered lump of tobacco clung to its tip.

Megha pressed her lips to suppress the oncoming nausea.

"That's not good for us," she said. "The tobacco. You should stop that."

Her older self ignored the remark and continued.

"I am also sure I won't be able to visit again. I think this was a one-time ticket."

"Hmm."

"Now that you have given every excuse and idea you could think of," Old Megha said. "Will you do this? For us? Learn to cook our food?"

"Hmm."

"Thank you. I promise you will understand the importance of it."

"Okay."

Old Megha checked the time on the wall clock.

"I will be pulled back soon."

"Wait…wait." Megha stood from the bed. "Do we get rich?"

"No."

"Oh. Then do we find our place in this…world? Do we fit well in the future?"

The old woman looked at her younger self with pity. She remembered a broken, insecure part of her from forty-five years ago.

"You will find your own band of misfits and outcasts, and then you won't be a misfit anymore. It's crazy how sometimes one fits much more nicely in a strange land than the land of their own."

Megha nodded. "Oh…we are like the Doctor!"

"What?"

"From *Doctor Who*. We are like the Doctor, traveling through time, only we don't have a Tardis. We have the clock."

The old woman glared at her.

"Hang on," Megha spoke again as another doubt hijacked her mind. "You were visited by yourself when you were twenty-one. Then why don't you remember this meet in the future?"

Old Megha gave it a long, deep thought. Then she gave a careless shrug.

"How meticulous," Megha mocked. "So what are you going to do now when you go back? Wait…Does this mean if I start learning to cook now, you will be able to make dal bhaat when you go back?"

"Hopefully."

"Fascinating."

"So…just food?" Megha spoke again. "I can't interfere with bigger events, but you have no other suggestions? Smaller changes you want me to make so that your life is better?"

"Just this. Oh, don't stop working out. We want to dance better."

"Dance?"

"Yes, we like dancing now."

"Not happening!"

A ticking sound resonated in Old Megha's ears—tick tock, tick tock.

"It's time. I have to leave."

Megha didn't reply.

"Hey!" The old woman clapped her hands in Megha's face.

"Sorry, I was thinking," Megha mumbled, looking at the floor. Something clicked in her head. "Do you remember we used to collect random junk from everywhere? We had a box full of those things."

"I don't remember many things these days." Old Megha coughed. "Why?"

"Just curious. Checking your memory. One more thing. You said we cannot change big events, just unimportant ones, like learning to cook. Right?"

"Right."

"What if, say, inspired by this conversation, I build a Tardis phone booth and wear its key around my neck all the time. Would you have that key around your neck when you reach the future again? Would you remember making the Tardis?"

Old Megha gave it a thought.

"I don't know. I don't do this on a daily basis, this time traveling."

"How unfortunate." Megha tapped her feet.

The tick-tock got louder.

"You are leaving in six months. Spend some time with Mummy and Pappa," Old Megha advised like a grandmother. "Don't stay cooped up here like a rat."

"Fine."

"Learn the patience to sit and read a book. It will serve you well in the later days."

"Okay," Megha replied, still distracted.

"Oh, I don't know if this is against the rules, but somewhere in your late thirties, you'll want to throw away your chai strainer. DON'T!"

"Uh, huh."

"They don't sell—" Before Old Megha could finish her sentence, she got plucked from the past and dropped back in the future.

The old woman looked around. It was her New York City apartment, just the way she had left it. She felt around her body to make sure she was okay and walked up to the clock. It was lying on the couch where she had dropped it before traveling. One hour had passed since she had left.

Behind the clock was a ticking timer that was counting down from five hours when she traveled to the past. She was sure the timer indicated the remaining time of her life. In four hours, she knew she was going to die.

Old Megha stood like a melting mannequin and tried to think of food, hoping to know how to cook dal bhaat, just like her mummy. Nothing appeared. Instead, another memory trickled into her head.

She was young, sitting in her childhood bedroom and dreaming about a life in the west when an old, scary woman appeared out of nowhere. She remembered the exact conversation they had, but this time, from the point of view of her younger self.

Old Megha trembled when she remembered what had happened after she, the sixty-six-year-old Megha, had left the room.

After she disappeared, young Megha grabbed a stool, opened a top storage cabinet, and pulled out a heavy, dusty box. It held things she had collected over the years. Duct tape, a compass, cogs and gears, grease in tiny bottles, screws, sandpaper, three screwdrivers, and dozens of tools and scraps. Below all of the junk was the star of the show—a vintage escapement that she had scored from Chor Bazaar, the infamous flea market of her city. She was on her usual hunt when she stumbled upon the mechanism lying in a mucky corner of a Victorian clock shop.

Young Megha had placed the box on her bed and searched, 'How to build a clock' on her laptop. On the second browser tab, she had filled out a school application form for the Horology program in New York.

"Hoarder of useless trivia, my ass," young Megha had sneered. "You are welcome, old, nasty, Megha."

In the forlorn home in the future, Old Megha's hand went to her mouth as she caught a new memory. She saw herself, a little younger than she was now but a lot older than twenty-one, drop the clock at the door of her apartment. A clock that she had built with her own hands.

"Woah…" she exclaimed, both impressed and terrified. Before she could get comfortable with this discovery, hundreds of other memories rained in her head, each like a meteor scratching through her mind and perforating the fabric of time and space.

She saw herself traveling through time, visiting all her past and future versions, and inflating the radius of her existence on the landscape of reality. She remembered breaking rules, making new ones, finding loopholes, and visiting times and eras that weren't even her own.

The old woman dropped on the couch. She thought her head was going to explode as she visualized her timeline in her head being crossed with zig-zag lines until nothing was left but scribbles.

Minutes later, when the downpour of memories subsided, her nostrils flared. She grew furious at the jad hu, bull-headed, twenty-one-year-old Megha for once again not doing something she was asked to do. Instead, she had abused the power and joggled her entire life.

Old Megha dug her elbows into her thighs and held her head.

Then, just like the last drop of a stormy rainfall or the last conscious second before a peaceful sleep, an important memory dripped into her mind—how to make perfect dal bhaat, just like her mummy.

2. ARE WE THERE YET?

"Are we there yet, Daddy?" my six-year-old daughter asks for the nth time since we started our trip.

The engine thrums under me as I move around in the cockpit, my head heavy from exhaustion. I can almost hear my mind shutting down. My eyes burn from the lack of sleep. I had finally convinced myself that I needed rest to safely commandeer a spaceship and was on the verge of sneaking in a nap when my daughter pinged me.

"Just thirteen more years, honey," I answer her on the radio and settle into my seat at the controls. The stars outside seem to blur as I focus on the conversation.

"Kay," she says. "Did you taste it?"

I take a sip from the thermos that my daughter had couriered from the residence deck. Too bad, I am late in muting myself, because she hears me spitting the warm beverage as soon as I drink it.

"Oh," she mutters.

I fail at mustering the energy needed to console her, so I stick to the polite truth. "Much better than the last time. You should be asleep by now. What are you doing?"

"Playing with the moon rock and thinking."

Four years ago, when I was the command module pilot for one of our space missions, I had landed on our moon and was allowed to keep a small rock we had collected from its surface. It's my daughter's most favorite thing in the universe. She loves it just as much as I love her.

"What are you thinking?" I ask her, almost regretting my question, and look again at the inviting rest tank to my left.

"About my flaws. Papa says I might be a baby, but I will be thirty years old when we reach the New Planet. I will not fit in if I can't make their beverage."

My husband is the loveliest being who would break the world in two for our daughter. However, there are three things I wish he knew. He is a top-notch pessimist, he could benefit from a bit of emotional intelligence, and he can't count to save his life. Not that I claim to be a great father. My attempts backfire, too. To boost our daughter's confidence and alleviate her anxiety regarding our relocation, I assigned her a small goal to accomplish—learning how to prepare the beverage of the aliens, our Hosts, who are providing us refuge on their planet.

"He says that because he is always worried about you," I tell her. "By the time we reach the New Planet, you will barely be twenty. Papa sucks at counting, honey."

"He says the same about me, that I can't even do those…those…adding and removing?"

"Math."

"Yes," my little one complains. "I can't even math. The aliens will hurt me."

I have to figure out the root cause of some of my daughter's fears, but for now, I let it slide from my mental notepad.

"No one is going to hurt you," I reassure. "How is your language learning going?"

"Bad," she answers without any embellishment.

"It's okay," I say. "They speak a lot of languages just like us, so you can try different ones and practice the one that's easy for you. We have a lot of time before we land. I will teach you some tomorrow, okay?"

"Kay."

"Go to sleep now." I rise from my seat and head toward the rest tank. "You have school tomorrow."

"It's hard for me at night, Daddy. Our home and the fights come to me in my dream. Why do I always feel scared? What if our Hosts don't take us?"

The thought of never having a home for our child crosses my mind again, and it infects my drowsiness, making it worse. My head pounds. It is only my emotional strength that keeps me going because, physically and mentally, I am more deteriorated than a diseased patient. If I have to talk for one more minute, I might scream.

"Is Papa with you?" I ask.

"No, he went to a meeting on the south deck. When are you coming to the cabin? Can I come there?"

"Honey, you can't be here, you know that. My shift will end in a few months. I will be in the cabin with you and Papa before you know it." Why did I have to make the rule of keeping the pilots separate from the other passengers? Maybe not all pilots get as emotionally charged and reckless after meeting their families as one of my colleagues who almost got us killed.

"Kay. It's just that I feel alone in life," she adds.

I. Just. Need. A. Few. Hours. Of. Sleep! Why is it an unattainable task?

I draw a deep breath and return to the controls. The glare from the metallic side panels pierces my eyes. "What about your friends?" I force myself to sip the beverage again, hoping the terrible, poison-like liquid will keep me awake. Its bitterness coats my throat as I swallow it, making my eyes twitch.

"They are not my friends. Dee said the Hosts would never talk to me because I cry a lot. Friends do not make fun of your emotions and feelings."

"No, they don't. Don't worry. One day, you'll make new friends on the New Planet."

I love my daughter, but all I want right now is for her to end the call so I can allow myself some respite.

"But that's so far away."

"Just thirteen more years," I say to her, diverting my gaze from the controls to peer into the vast expanse of space. Doubts assail me once more. What if this isn't the most rational course? I will be fifty-five years old when we arrive. My husband will be fifty-one. The thought terrifies me. But I remind myself we aren't undertaking this journey for ourselves. We are doing it for our children, who deserve a brighter future than the one we left behind on our home planet. She deserves to inhabit a kinder world. We all do. I didn't spend a year persuading my community to undertake this move, only to second-guess my own decision now. They elected me as their commander, placing their lives in my hands, and I must live up to that trust.

"Go to the window. I'll tell you a story." I say to my daughter as I drag my lifeless body toward my own window on the side of the cockpit. "But then you sleep, alright?"

"Yes!" Her voice brims with excitement, followed by the sound of flapping. She loves stories.

"What do you see outside?" I ask her.

"Faint stars, Daddy. But mostly dark…" I hear her stretching against the window of our cabin. "Aaeeh…the glass is so cold."

"Be careful."

She does not respond to my request, but I am certain she must have quickly nodded three times like she always does.

"Look at the backside," I add. "Can you spot the tail of our ship?"

"I can! Is that where the hurt ones are?"

"Yes, that's where the hospital is," I reply, attempting to avoid thoughts of the alien species who had invaded our planet. I, too, elongate my body to peek at our cabin through the window. But I know I can't; I tried on the day we lifted off.

"Daddy…"

"Yes, honey."

"I can see our sun. Far, far away."

"That's not our sun," I remark, looking at the same flickering star she is observing. It reminds me of all the nights when I'd clutched my telescope, glided to our rooftop, and lost myself in the night sky for hours. My stomach churns. I had always assumed that if I were ever in space again, it would be to explore the vastness of the universe and unveil new worlds, not to escape from our own home.

I look back at the star and experience a pang of sympathy for it. Despite its magnificent luminosity, colossal size, and unfathomable power, it remains tethered, unable to escape even if it desires to. It's one place where we mortals triumph over these celestial bodies we so greatly admire. "That's Heztu," I explain. "A star much bigger than our sun."

My daughter does not reply, so I ask, "Ready for the story?"

"I miss home." Her voice comes low. "I miss my school, my play tank. We left everything. I miss Flora a lot, too. She cannot come alive?"

My heart punctures at her last question. I remember why sleep eludes me and nightmares stalk me. Hundreds of parents of our planet did not agree to make this toiling thirteen-year journey for pleasure.

Two years ago, the Huzweal galaxy invaders seized our planet. They had depleted their energy, and initially, they aimed to harness it from us adults. But soon, they discovered a horrifying alternative—our children could be subjected to partial integration with their physiology and transformed into living generators. Numerous of our children were ruthlessly taken. They would emerge a few days later, looking more like the Huzwealian species than our own offspring.

It was then that I conceived the daring escape plan. With only a single functional spaceship at our disposal, we couldn't save everyone. Tragically, the worst transpired. Desperate parents, driven to the brink, turned on each other to secure a seat on the ship. More violence and deaths, but this time, among our own. I don't blame them; who could watch their own children turn into soulless automatons?

To avoid a bigger civil conflict, which could have alerted the aliens, we decided to flee weeks earlier than planned. As one of the few capable of piloting a spaceship, I faced the task of deciding which families would board and which would be left behind. An experience I wouldn't wish on any soul.

My family and others secretly boarded the ship, holding our children tightly. However, not all parents were so fortunate. Flora was taken the night before our departure. I had to tell my daughter that she had passed away in her sleep. It took her days to overcome the initial shock, and to think I was wondering about the root cause of my daughter's fears. She has more than one.

Now, I can't shake the haunting images of my own child facing a similar fate.—her lovely face, partly metal, her gentle, beautiful soul, partly wires. The mere thought causes me to lose my grasp on the window's glass, and I tumble to the floor, a plopping sound reverberating in the cockpit.

As I rise, I say, "I am sorry for everything, honey." Exhaustion had me in a grip so firm that I had not been completely present while talking to my daughter. Shame and regret smack me in the gut. "I understand how much you miss your school, our home, and Flora. But we will have a better, much safer home on the New Planet. I promise. No more running and hiding."

"Will they be nice to me? The new aliens?"

Of course. How can anyone not be nice to someone like my daughter?

Well, others proved me wrong. I don't bask in that delusion anymore. But I say, "Why wouldn't they? They are very kind. I have heard great stories about them."

"What stories?"

"Heartwarming stories." I reflect on everything I've learned about the species discovered by one of our astronomers many years ago. When we could no longer resist the Huzwealians, they were the first to come to my mind. Establishing contact with them took tremendous effort. How would you even make first contact with an alien species living light-years away? Nevertheless, we persevered. Once we made initial contact, they generously shared a wealth of information about themselves and their planet—details about their existence, history, dietary habits, survival strategies, population, and more. I thought we were an overcrowded planet, but their staggering number stunned me.

Having been chosen as our spokesperson, I engaged in frequent communication with one of their representatives. There were language barriers, but as soon as we built the translators, I informed them about our crisis. Their deliberation took time, but they ultimately concluded they had enough space and resources to home us. Only they had one condition. We must come in peace.

Our history proves we are not a peaceful civilization. We couldn't even extend kindness to our species, but of course, we had to go in peace. What other options did we have? The inhabitants of the New Planet far surpass us in intelligence, making any attempt at confrontation futile, a fact they are well aware of. They know more about us than we know about them. A much-advanced civilization.

I ponder it all and consider stories that might comfort my distressed daughter.

"Do you know," I begin, "this alien species…well, there are multiple species on their planet, but our current communication is with just one of them. They are older than we are and yet have survived. Their ways are weird, but one thing remains clear—they are compassionate. They hold a high regard for all forms of life. Do you know they also faced a catastrophic event? A couple of hundred years ago. A raging fire."

"Oh…and then what happened?"

"They rallied together and survived. The ones who weren't affected gave everything they had to save, feed, and shelter the ones who suffered. Some even died saving others."

"Wow."

The surprise in my daughter's response made me think of our past. Our ancestors once followed a similar path, being there for one another, but now, we compile lists to determine who deserves to survive. Sacrificing our own needs for the benefit of others has become such a foreign concept that I cannot even imagine ourselves doing what the Hosts are undertaking for us.

It dawns upon me that I haven't spoken in a while, yet my daughter stays quiet and patient on the other side, knowing well the ill conversational habits of her daddy.

"So, yes, honey," I speak. "They are a weird, alien species, but they are committed to one another. I'd rather be that than be normal and unkind."

"Me too. But how can they be so nice without the reward system? Papa says they don't have a reward system."

"They don't do niceness for selfish rewards. You know how you get stars when you help your classmates? And you can buy nice things with those stars?"

"Yes? I always get the most number of stars. But I do not do it just for stars, daddy."

"I know, honey. But these species, they also don't do it for stars. Instead of rewards, they get a fresh doze of good chemicals poured into their bodies. That encourages them to help more."

"But that *is* the reward," my intelligent daughter refutes.

"Yes, but they probably aren't aware of it."

"Kay," she considers. "Do they have friendships, Daddy?"

"Of course they do. Much deeper friendships than ours. Their civilization depends and thrives on it."

"Do they also live on a ball-like planet like ours?"

"Yes, but it's sort of self-aware, their planet. It recycles itself and wears a powerful armor to sustain itself and the life on it."

"I cannot imagine that in my mind."

"We will see it with our eyes soon."

"Daddy, did you know one of Papa's friends from C deck believes these aliens eat with their noses?" My daughter giggles.

"That must be the wisecracker, Sunny?"

"Yes!"

"Well, he is not completely wrong."

"Really? Eating with noses? Both air and food? Dirty."

I imagine my daughter's contorted head.

"It's a part of their biology, honey."

"Do they also have the same food as we do?" She asks another question.

"Not exactly. Their food comes in bizarre forms; we are not even familiar with some of those forms. It might be a bit challenging at first, but our scientists assure us that whatever they eat will also sustain us. Isn't that remarkable? A completely alien species, residing light-years away from us, yet we can thrive on similar sustenance." Something about what I say eases my anxiety.

"Very magical. But they look scary. Our teacher showed us a picture of them. They have so many holes in their body, and Daddy, their bottoms! How can they move on that? They must keep falling."

I laugh. Somewhere on the New Planet, if a parent is talking to their child about us, they must be discussing our anatomy. I look at the reflection of my own body on the window, a form we've been accustomed to for so long, we don't even realize it might appear peculiar to others. I hope they are sharing a laugh about us as well. It's better to be found funny than scary.

"They move alright," I say.

"If our body parts are so different, how will I tell my new friends that I like them? They do not even have an ear."

"They hear but differently. They also use strange but amusing gestures to express. Like if they are sad, they dribble soothing oil and mucus from their body and if they are happy their bones contract, making loud sounds. When they meet someone, they create collisions."

"That's funny." My daughter laughs this time, a healing balm for my headache.

"Do you know they wake up tall and become shorter by the time they go back to sleep? And they change a thousand different skins throughout their lifetime?"

"I think that is creepy but also cool."

We fall into a moment of silence, both of us observing the dark space outside our windows. I sense my little one coming up with a question that's been on her mind for a while. That's what she does. She'll share all her fears, children-fears, and then astound me with something that makes me forget she is only six. My daughter has an old soul, and at times, she steps into the role of a parent in my life.

"Daddy."

"Yes, honey."

"Are you afraid?"

"Why do you ask?"

"Because you are always very brave."

I understand why she thinks that might be the reason for someone to be afraid. Being brave is a solitary task, especially when you are in my position. Involuntary solitude often leaves you alone and afraid. My daughter might not be good at math, but she is terrific at adding up emotions.

"Yes, I am afraid sometimes. We had to leave our home, lose our loved ones, and now we are going to this new world we had never seen before. But it's normal to feel that way. Fear helps us survive. It's okay to imagine the worst because we have lived the worst."

"But Papa says you don't imagine the worst at all; you are too positive. He says it's sus…suspisas, that the aliens are only good, that they don't have any bad qualities."

I chuckle and shake my head, thinking about my husband. It's been so long since I've heard him say that to my face. I miss him more than I convey to him every day.

"Of course, they do," I reply to my daughter. "They have a dark history, too, just like ours. But they didn't give up. They united, learned from their mistakes, and remained resilient. We almost went extinct because we couldn't figure out how to work together. We believe we are an evolved species, but we still have so much growing to do. Maybe these aliens will teach us that, and that's why I am positive."

"But we still know us. We don't know them."

"I know, honey. But sometimes familiarity can hurt, and the unknown can bring comfort. Would we have offered refuge, a home to someone from a strange planet without even meeting them? The Hosts are doing that for us."

"How can I learn to trust them so much, the way you trust them?"

"You don't have to. Trust is earned. They have earned mine. You don't have to trust them like I do until you know them well, okay?"

"Kay. They will not separate me from you? I will stay with you and Papa?"

"You will always stay with us. A compassionate species will never separate children from their parents. They won't.

No one has the courage to separate me from you, honey. Not even them."

As I utter these noble words to my daughter, I find myself sinking deeper into the 'well of dangerous optimism,' a term my husband often uses to describe me. Once more, I hope, as I have countless times, that my positivity doesn't bring harm to my family or our group. I am crossing galaxies with the belief that these alien species are different from those who invaded us. That they won't kill us, separate us, or experiment on us. I desperately hope my faith won't become the catastrophe that drives our species to extinction.

The fluids inside seem to gurgle. But then I hear my daughter again.

"You always know how to make my heart better."

"So do you."

"I can't wait to go to the new home and play with you. I will tell Papa to not worry and have safe feelings," my sweet daughter says, for she doesn't know what her beloved papa, my husband, had seen nights before we left. He had been through more frightening times than I have, and I cannot wait for him to have faith again, too.

It's strange. In this quest of life, a home should be the default. A constant safe space from where we step out, face the uncertainties of life and return. Yet we spend our whole lives finding a safe home. I try not to ponder over it and respond to my daughter.

"Thank you, my precious."

"I worry about you too, Daddy. Are you taking the medicine? You work very hard for others but not for yourself."

"I am taking the medicine."

"Are your emotions okay?"

"They are okay. They are strong, but they are okay." I clasp a bottle from a drawer of my belongings and chug some of my medicine.

"I miss you very much," my daughter says and then sings. She chirps a melody she has hummed many times before, and it shatters me. My child has done this on more occasions than I can remember, but something about today, about this time, rattles me. I feel strong yet fragile. I feel fragile, yet strong. I try to suppress it, but a sob erupts out of me. My burdens melt into the honeyed sounds of my six-year-old. I remind myself that I would do anything to protect her.

"Oh, Daddy." She stops mid-singing. "What if I never learn their language? How am I going to talk to them? They don't speak our tongue."

I compose myself and thank the universe for my daughter's inquiring mind, for her questions always keep me distracted from the harsh realities of life.

"Do you know," I say, "if they were listening to our conversation right now, they would understand us?"

"How?"

"After they sent their languages to us, our scientists created translators and installed them in our bodies. So even when we speak in our language, the Hosts will hear it in theirs. Isn't that remarkable?"

"Is that why Papa took me to the doctor?"

"Yes."

"Very magical."

"Alright, it's late now," I say, checking the time. "School tomorrow. It's time to get some sleep."

"One last question. Please!" she pleads, drawing out the word for seconds.

I laugh. "Go on."

"Do we have to create collisions too when we meet them?"

"You don't have to. But yes, I will..." I check the term the Hosts use for this greeting, "hug them."

"Okay. I won't create a hug in the start."

"That's fine, honey."

"Can you tell Papa to get more coffee grounds from the lab so I can keep trying coffee?"

"Sure. We will make it together once I am back at the cabin."

"I treasure you, Daddy."

"I treasure you too. Give Papa a kiss for me."

"I will."

My daughter goes off the air. I take a deep breath and remove the radio from my ear, or as the Hosts amusingly call it, 'scalp pocket.' My dozen fins flap violently as I float to my seat. The scales on my body fade from deep brown to beige as my emotions subside. I imagine my daughter's beautiful bright red scales turning orange as she relaxes in her tank for the night.

I glance at my own rest tank, but the telescope next to it beckons me. Peering through its eyepiece, I stare into the boundless depths of space. I maneuver it to observe our destination.

My dorsal fin flutters above me as I spot the third planet of what they call the solar system. A blue marbled ball, our New Planet of hope and our new home. Its inhabitants, our kind Hosts—one of its million living species—the humans, call it Earth.

3. GAME TRANSFER PHENOMENA

If I die, and I am being generous, Raccoony. If I die, you have seven days to mourn. After that, you must live an even better life," Naksh had told a trembling Araaia a week before he died. She had awakened him, like many nights before, seeking solace for a panic attack she couldn't face alone.

"If I die, and I am not going to be generous," she had declared when her tears had evaporated from his warm chest and diffused with the humidity of their tiny, coastal-town apartment. "You have seven days to get your things in order. Then you are coming after me."

Now Naksh had been dead for fifteen days, but Araaia could neither live a better life nor follow him. She had always thought of herself as a brave woman, but if she was, she would have slit her wrist or overdosed herself, for death was more enticing than living with the absence of her husband of four years.

She stared at a small rectangular box, the size of a big book, sitting by the foot of her couch. Inside it was the one remaining cure. Inside it was her husband.

November 14, 2045

Araaia slipped into a pair of jeans, a shirt, and old shoes. Days had passed since she last wore outside clothes. But there were numerous emails from Naksh's employer since he had died. They were offering their products and that's all she needed to leave her house.

The moment she set foot on the street, she froze. Unconcerned faces swept past, conveying that her world had halted but not theirs. It had always been evident to her that she was an outsider, but the fact that the trees, cars, birds, and air moved just as they did before Naksh's death alienated her from the world more than ever.

She rubbed her chin on her shoulder, gawking around. Her knees swayed, but her feet refused to budge. Even though no one glanced at her, she imagined the passersby shaking their heads at her pitiable state. *Get a grip,* she heard them say.

Araaia turned around and retreated back home.

The apartment hit her on the other cheek, its lonely corners reaching out to strangle her. It had been a week since her husband's death, but time moved slowly in this corner of her universe.

She scanned the house with swollen eyes, encountering fragments of memories scattered everywhere. In the kitchen, she was standing beside Naksh, pouring orange juice into her quarter-gallon glass while he made himself his everyday breakfast. On the couch, they sat side by side for hours, their bodies touching and basking in a comfortable silence. Near the window, they were celebrating cleaning their house by gripping their hands together and doing an arm wave. On the living room floor, their heads rested on each other's, watching TV.

On her desk, she was dramatically muttering, "I hate Naksh," shoving the lamp in her face, feigning torment like a tortured prisoner, and then screaming, "Fine, fine. I confess, I love him!" From the couch, Naksh laughs, shakes his head, and calls her a Raccoonic Idiot.

A chilly draft roused Araaia, vaporizing the fragments around the house. She wiped her cheeks, flung off her shoes, and peeled away her jeans. From a narrow rack, which was Naksh's closet, she snatched one of his sweaters. His remaining clothes lay strewn on the floor, each garment sniffed until its scent vanished. Donning the sweater, she settled in front of her computer, her sunken, overused chair cradling her hip.

Naksh had urged her countless times to switch to lenses so she could work and play from anywhere, but Araaia liked her computer big and tangible. With the lenses, the games she played and wrote seemed too real for her taste, and unconsciously, she had always feared the blurred line between two realities—hers and the virtual.

She turned on the computer. Nine emails. All from work. She was in the middle of drafting characters for her company's new role-playing game. The deadline was only three weeks away.

They could wait. Her husband had just died.

Araaia then navigated to Naksh's employer's website, Gadget gAIa. After thirty minutes of browsing, a voice chimed in her ears.

"This is one of our premium AR products, the baddest of all, AI4PRO."

Through her VR glasses, Araaia watched the salesperson point at a console over a well-lit table.

"What's the difference?" she asked.

"Not only does it possess self-awareness and human-level intelligence," the salesperson asserted, "but unlike other models, this one evolves and ages, just like humans. It will absorb all the cognitive data from your husband's brain—memories and all that mental jazz. We will have you answer a few questions to help us tighten the Incarnate—that's what we call them—and voila! Pure human. Only without flesh and bones. And let's admit it, those are the grossest parts." He winked.

Araaia stared deeper into the salesperson's eyes, wondering if he, too, was an Incarnate.

"How does the aging work?" she asked, forgetting for a second the huge hole in her chest.

"For physical elements, we will use his DNA, genetic code, and medical history. This will help the Incarnate age physically, mirroring your husband's natural progression. Drawing from surveillance and virtual records—his emails, photos, videos, and social media—the AI4PRO will adopt his quirks, habits, lingo, facial expressions, and then factor in age and growth rate. Think of it as simulating human evolutionary psychology but on a highly personalized level. Wondrous, isn't it?"

Araaia wanted to respond, but her words seemed to get stuck in her throat. Engaging in verbal conversation turned out to be more draining than she had anticipated. It was the first time she had spoken to someone since before Naksh's cremation. The sound of a human voice alone grated on her eardrums.

"Okay," she managed to utter.

"Not just that," the salesperson said, raising his finger. "It will also remember life incidents and lessons. For example, if your husband knocked his head on a cabinet door, his Incarnate will remember to close that freakin' overhead cabinet next time!"

"Will it be…sentient?"

"Yes. It will perceive and experience all emotions, but at the same threshold as your husband would."

"Will you accept payment through three different accounts?"

Finances were an issue. Araaia had donated most of Naksh's money to Forge Ahead, a small group her husband secretly supported. An aspiring rebel force, they helped people cope with grief and loss without the help of Gadget gAIa products, the company where Naksh had to work to earn his living. The cost of AI4PRO would leave Araaia with close to nothing in her bank. She reminded herself that she had to wake up every morning, no matter what, and keep her job.

"Wondrous! And yes, we do!" The salesperson clicked his heels. "Ah, you are lucky, lucky, lucky! We have a holiday-offer. With the purchase of AI4PRO, you get the Customization feature for free!"

"What's that?"

"Why, it's a customization of your choosing, of course. You can remove a habit you didn't like in your partner, a pet peeve that bothered you," the salesperson brought his face closer to the camera and cupped his hand over his mouth, "They all have one. He kept interrupting while you played Clustersky? Make him less nosey. He liked everything neat and organized? Make him a little messy. It's free!"

If Arraia didn't already know how Gadget gAIa operates, she might have wondered how the salesperson knew she played Clustersky or about her need for hyper-privacy while playing games or her diabolical untidiness.

Contemplating the customization feature reminded her of the last argument with Naksh. He had always despised how little she cared about her well-being. She never exercised or went out with people or ate healthily. In fact, Araaia would often jest about how no one enjoyed those activities except Naksh, prompting a very Naksh-like response from him.

"That's because everyone is playing into the hands of Gadget gAIa. They want us despondent and depressed so they can capitalize on it. We need to fight them by doing what they don't want us to do."

His indefatigable attitude had never sat right with Araaia. What else?

Naksh also had annoying habits, such as stretching all the time, even while he was sitting on the couch, or taking his sweet time getting ready, or walking too fast when they walked together, leaving her behind. He also had a tendency to become too cold and straightforward when he didn't agree with something. Plus, he had unreasonable, high standards for himself and others, which to Araaia seemed more unfair than everything else

She scratched the tattoo on the side of her palm. It read "Create." Then, she placed her hands back on the keyboard out of habit.

"I don't need the customization feature," she said. "Just make it exactly like him."

"Wondrous! AI4PRO will also feature a manual function, denoted by the green M on the dashboard. You can input scenarios, emotions, events—anything and anyway you like, and your augmented reality will bring it to life. Role-play your life away!"

"Okay."

"Remember, you cannot kill an Incarnate; it's against the law. They all live out their natural years, calculated based on people's medical records. Your husband's health suggests he would have lived up to..." the salesperson squinted, "seventy-one years old. Woah! That's one healthy human. Most customers live up to sixty."

Araaia scratched her desk until it chipped her nails.

"We will send you the questionnaire, if you could fill it up ASAP."

"Okay."

"You will receive the order within twenty-four hours."

"Okay."

"Do you want the Incarnate to know it's an Incarnate?"

Naksh had started working for Gadget gAIa over three years ago when he couldn't find any other option to secure their apartment. Over the years, he had understood their work and had loathed them from the core of his being. Living through a jungle of cables and chips after death is abuse, he had said. Just before he died, he had shared with Araaia about how he wanted to quit his job and do something meaningful, something that heals people and does not encourage them to stay ill.

"Mademoiselle," the salesperson almost squealed. "Do you want the Incarnate to know it's an Incarnate? Most people like that. It gives them a sense of power."

"No."

"Thank you for the business. Have a wondrous day, Araaia!"

As Araaia ended the call, a drunken cackle droned from the neighbor's place. How could they dare to laugh when the person with the most magical laughter had been snatched from the world?

The arrival of the questionnaire helped dissipate her momentary rage. Filling it wouldn't be difficult. She knew Naksh better than the back of her hand.

Reading the questions, she answered them.

How would you describe him in three words?
Altruistic, Pragmatic, Devoted
What was his favorite food?
French fries
What did he call you?
Raccoony
What was he scared of?
Being vulnerable. And spiders. It also scared him a great deal when I jumped out of nowhere to prank him, although he never admitted to it.
What was his biggest fear?

Falling into an illness that won't allow him to work or grow. He didn't like being stuck in one place. Staying the same person was his biggest nightmare.

Araaia continued answering the questions, her eyeballs bulging out of two dark holes. She drank orange juice, carton after carton, mopping her mouth with Naksh's sweater after each sip.

What was his biggest regret?

Taking up a job that didn't align with his values

What would he do if he made a mistake no one saw?

He'd act the same way he would've acted if someone saw him making a mistake

What would he do if you upset him?

He'd go on a run to clear his mind and then come back to calmly communicate his concerns with me

What would he do if he tumbled while walking?

Be upset with himself for not walking properly

What would he do if he broke a glass on the floor?

He would threaten me to not move from my spot until he cleaned it

From 1 to 10, how do you rate his intelligence?

9

From 1 to 10, how do you rate his emotional intelligence?

7

From 1 to 10, how would you rate his intellectual growth rate?

10

From 1 to 10, how would you rate his emotional growth rate?

6

Listener or solver?

Solver

Left or right-brained?

Left

Thinker or feeler?

Both

What made him laugh?

My random skits and his own jokes

What made him cry?

The pain of the helpless and abused

What did he hate most?

Apathy, dormancy, and cruelty

What did he love most?

Me

Araaia had spent two hours completing the questionnaire, feeling as if Gadget gAIa had some sort of vendetta against her. It forced her to remember all the little aspects of her husband that made him whole. She had cried, and she had filled in the answers.

Now, eight days later, the unopened package at the foot of the couch stared back at her. She pushed away the empty juice cartons and microwave meal boxes with her feet and cleared the space around it. With her heart thumping inside her chest, she picked up the box, sliced the tape with a box cutter, and peered inside.

The AI4PRO kit looked similar to her gaming console. However, this one had a set of contacts, a haptic bodysuit, and a pair of gloves.

Araaia plugged in the console and put on the contacts and gloves. She stripped naked and slid inside the haptic bodysuit. The black jumpsuit engulfed her body from the neck to the toes. In an alternate universe where Naksh was still alive, she would have jumped around the room, pretending to be a ninja or a cartoon character, uttering video game sounds. Her husband would have cackled and called her a Raccoonic idiot.

'Are you ready?'

The letters hung in the middle of the room. Seated at her desk, she touched '**Yes**' in the air.

A waiver appeared, and she scrolled through it until she reached the last clause.

'Killing an Incarnate is illegal. According to our data, this Incarnate will live up to the age of 71 years.'

Araaia agreed to the terms and signed her name. The screen went blank.

She took a weak breath.

Before she exhaled, a body materialized in front of her— an Incarnate, as Gadget gAIa called it.

Naksh's face stared back.

Araaia thrust from her seat, sending the chair sliding behind. She scratched her arms and fell to her knees.

The Incarnate's frozen head jerked, the lines and creases on its face moved, and its body turned and curved.

"Raccoony," came the familiar, deep voice that struck the darkest chords of her soul. The Incarnate's brows lifted just as Naksh's did when he used to say her name like that. It looked behind at the kitchen and then around as if it was lost.

Araaia's eyes filled up. She jumped at the image of her husband.

"Naksh!" A whimper came through an explosion of tears as she smooshed her head into the Incarnate's chest. The oddness of it all rubbed in when she felt Naksh's back through her gloves and his body through her suit, but not his weight or his scratchy stubble on her face.

Her husband's voice alone, however, was enough to stall the soul-crushing pain she had felt since he died.

"Awh…" The Incarnate bent from the knees and hunched its body to hug just like Naksh because he was a foot taller than Araaia. "You okay?"

She could only nod.

"What day is it?" it asked. Before Araaia could answer, the Incarnate laughed and said, "Look at that. I always made fun of you for forgetting what day it is."

Araaia didn't want to talk or stop listening to Naksh's voice. But the Incarnate didn't know it was an Incarnate.

"It's Saturday, November twenty-second."

"Huh." It jolted its face backward. "Strange. Two weeks passed quickly."

The Incarnate had all the memories of Naksh until the day before he died.

Araaia couldn't help but stare at its face. She caressed its stubble and moved her fingers through its thick, black hair, her gloved fingers tingling with sensation. The hole inside her chest puffed with fuzzy vapor.

"What's wrong? Why are you crying?" The image of her husband held her shoulders and peered into her eyes. "Another of those panic attacks? I am not going anywhere,

Raccoony." It wrapped its arm around her neck. "I am meant to live a long, weird life with you."

Araaia let out a loud sob.

Naksh was her sounding board, for the world outside, she thought, was deaf to her. There weren't many things she hadn't shared with him. Now she was carrying a heavy secret inside her, and the helplessness of not being able to share it shattered her.

"Coffee?" the Incarnate asked, knowing it was something she loved but found too time-consuming to make, unlike orange juice.

It knows, Araaia thought, experiencing a familiar sense of comfort.

When Naksh's image went into the kitchen, she understood why Gadget gAIa had updated her apartment. Every appliance, every device, every piece of furniture was connected to the sensory output of the Incarnate, making it augmented into Araaia's reality.

The image turned on the electric coffee maker and began to brew a cup of coffee. Araaia removed her contacts. The kitchen was empty. Ghostly. She wore them back and watched as the output from the Incarnate triggered the appliances in her kitchen.

A few minutes later, the image returned with a plate of French fries and a cup of coffee in its hand. Araaia removed the contacts again and saw that the coffee was steaming in a cup under the coffee maker.

She understood the process.

When Naksh's image offered her the coffee, she pretended to accept the virtual beverage. Then she paused the Incarnate and walked to the kitchen to grab the real cup. It was a matter of pretense and imagination, just like her games. She could have left the real coffee alone, and the Incarnate would have continued seeing the augmented cup in its reality, but she wanted to drink the beverage. It was Naksh's selfless gesture of love, his simple language of solicitude. It didn't matter that it came from a snippet of him.

She sat next to the Incarnate, placing her thighs on its lap, wrapping her arms around its neck, and laying down her head on its shoulder. To an observer, if there was one in the room, she sat alone, her legs dangling from the couch, her arms circled around an empty space, and her body in a brief slant. Araaia had always been a keen observer of herself throughout her life. She knew this in the back of her mind, the fact that she was leaning toward nothingness. It reminded her again that Naksh was gone, and this was just a lingering fragment of his identity.

"Weren't we supposed to go on a hike today?" the Incarnate asked.

Araaia remembered their plans. They were supposed to volunteer for a Forge Ahead initiative, where they incorporated nature excursions in groups to help the members deal with their grief.

"I don't feel like doing it. Can we just stay here, please?"

The Incarnate looked at Araaia's face, worried. It scooched closer to her and pulled her into its arms.

"Of course."

November 23, 2045

"You did what?" Sim's voice came through the headphones. He was Naksh's childhood and Araaia's only friend, who lived four thousand miles away.

"I got his Incarnate."

"From his employer?"

"Yes."

"Who else knows about this?"

"The Incarnate's perimeter ends at our apartment door. Once it tries to leave the house, it enters virtual reality and only meets the VR versions of the people and places he knows. So no one needs to know."

"Araaia, did you even talk to your family since he passed away?"

"No."

"I talked with your sister. You are not even answering their calls?"

Araaia stayed mum.

"This is not…"

"I know what they'll say," she interrupted. "Stop being sad, you need to move on, he is in a better place…the quintessential generic consolations that neither make me feel better nor help my…I can't move on. He is all I know and love. His better place was here! With me, in this house."

"I know." Sim sighed. "Did you at least talk to any of your friends?"

"I don't have any."

"Then what am I?"

A friend Araaia got through Naksh without putting in any work.

"Sorry. I…"

"I get it, Araaia. This sucks. But as cliché as it sounds, it's true. You *have* to move on. Maybe not now. Take your time, but you have to."

"I will."

"You need to talk to your family, to me, real people. Or sign up for Forge Ahead. You know Naksh trusted them more than anyone."

"I can't go outside right now."

"Then don't go outside, but this Incarnate, Araaia, it's not healthy. They damage humanity." Sim was one of the few people who held that opinion about Incarnates; he wouldn't have been Naksh's friend otherwise. "Naksh is gone," he added. "Some combination of codes is not going to replace him."

No one knows that more than her, she thought. Then said, "I can't survive in a world where he is not in it."

"That's not true. You have lived alone all your life before you met him. You have always enjoyed your space."

"That's not the same. This aloneness, it's tainted by his absence."

"Listen…"

"I need him to live through the tangible hours, even if it means he has to linger in a spectrum we don't call reality."

"He wouldn't have liked this."

"He wouldn't know."

"Araaia, you can't do this to him."

"Then he shouldn't have died."

December 1, 2045

Araaia lay awake next to the Incarnate, listening to its peaceful snores. She had spent a week with it, but other than its appearance evoking intense emotions within her, it wasn't bringing the solace she had hoped for.

As the streetlights' halogens flashed on its face, she gazed at its features. It looked exactly like Naksh, not a crease or hair out of place. Even its breathing mirrored his, chest rising and falling with the same rhythm. Yet, the constant awareness that she was alone in this house, on this bed, lingered.

Pulling her knees toward, she placed her arm under her head, the other hand yearning to caress the Incarnate's hair. She shuffled closer. Naksh used to ridicule her claim that she could identify his scent in a field full of people. But it was true. Even though he was gone, she remembered his smell, just like one would remember a memory.

Araaia breathed in less than a foot away from its face. Nothing emanated. She moved closer, tempted to kiss it all around.

"Kiai!" the image exclaimed.

Araaia jumped in fear. Her heart grew twice its size as she observed what it was doing. It was as if the world's best gift had jumped out of a scary box.

The Incarnate, just like Naksh, had propped his head, elbow, and knee forward as if to block Araaia from touching him.

"Are you doing your defense thing?" Araaia asked.

"Yes. Enemy detected," it announced in a robotic tone, just like her husband used to. "Naksh's Shell Defense activated. You can't breach these perimeters."

Araaia chuckled. "I'll crack this cheap shell in no time." She thrust her palm between the Incarnate's hands, mimicking a karate move, and tickled his neck.

Naksh's defense melted. He retracted his head, arms, and knees, breaking into laughter. "Stop!"

For a moment, Araaia wondered how the Incarnate perceived the tickling. Then she dismissed the thought to Gadget gAIa and continued her playful assault.

"You know I…" Naksh wriggled into a ball of laughter, "can't handle this. Stop." He grabbed her hands. "First, you wake me up by sniffing me like a dog, and now you do this…you wickedest fiend!"

Araaia cackled, the sound echoing in the empty room.

He cupped her head and leaned in for a kiss. Reality struck Araaia. Despite the illusion of him, she couldn't sense his presence on her face. Nevertheless, she played along. Her lips moved against the Incarnate. He grabbed her waist, pulling her closer.

Araaia writhed alone on the bed like a worm on hot asphalt until she moaned and drifted into sleep with eyes full of tears.

"You wouldn't believe this," Naksh's image gnarled as he entered the house. "Gadget gAIa stole the life data of some of the employees to build characters for their standard Incarnates."

Araaia wore her contacts upon hearing his voice.

"About time they have standard Incarnates with proper character arcs," Araaia mocked.

"Mind-sucking fuckers." Naksh dropped his bag. "I talked with a couple of people on my team. We are all going to quit next year."

Araaia sat at her desk, attempting to focus on her job assignment, due this week. She couldn't comprehend how Naksh had different stories from work every day, even though he was going to his job in virtual reality. For the first few days, she didn't let him go outside, but Naksh got suspicious. A bit upset even. So she thought, why not. This would give her a chance to finish some of her own work.

She wished to copy Gadget gAIa's approach—stealing cognitive, personal, and emotional data of real people. It clashed with her creative principles, but as she sat at her computer attempting to craft characters for their latest game, hours passed with nothing to show. That had never happened before. Her mind had always been a hub of ideas.

At least she was happy, she thought. Her husband was with her now.

Naksh approached her, huffing and rolling his sleeves. He bent and kissed her on the head, as he always did after coming home.

"I am going for a run. You wanna join?" he asked.

"No. You go ahead. I need to finish this."

"Okay."

"Come here." Araaia put her work aside and beckoned him to her chair. His distressed face still held the charm of the man she had fallen for years ago, his eyes still kinder than any pair she had ever seen.

She pulled him into a tight embrace and made a gritting face.

"I want to crush you into powder and snort you every day."

Naksh laughed, his frown lines disappearing.

"Raccoonic idiot."

December 31, 2045

Araaia shuffled closer to Naksh, yearning for a comforting embrace. She wrapped her hand around his sleeping image and brought her face, the only part of her body not covered in the haptic body suit, next to his lips. How she longed to experience Naksh's touch on her skin, the warmth she felt when he used to kiss her beneath the eyes.

Moving even closer, she shaped her fingers like lips and pressed them against her cheeks, her mind's eye, imagining it to be her husband. Then she clutched Naksh's lifeless image. It was like holding an empty box. The Incarnate, after all, was just a hollow shell of Naksh's data.

A lump formed in her throat, so tough it burned when she swallowed. To her surprise, her eyes didn't produce tears. She shut them once more, resting her face on Naksh's pillow, and imagined his weight in her arms. It was lighter than her guilt.

January 23, 2046

"Come on, move your limbs, Raccoony," Naksh urged. "The world is brimming with stagnant humans. Gadget gAIa wants us to be like this: motionless lumps clinging to their version of reality. We have to resist. Come on." He clapped his hands. "Switch off your game and eat something. Take a shower, write your book, call your sister."

Araaia chugged the stale, bitter orange juice and wiped her mouth with the hoodie she wore over the haptic bodysuit. Its zipper grazed the corner of her lip. She licked the wound and resumed her game.

Hot blisters had formed on her hand and other parts of the body from wearing the suit and gloves permanently. The contacts burned her eyes.

"Are you even listening to me, Araaia?"

She blinked, shook her palms, and stared back at the screen.

April 02, 2046

"You wanna play a round of Clustersky with me?" Araaia asked, her body curved like a crescent moon on the chair.

"Can you pause that for a second?" Naksh said. "We need to talk."

"Go on," she said, still looking at her screen.

"Pause and look here, Araaia." His voice was stern but not aggressive.

"Sorry. What's up?"

"We should split."

Araaia shook her head.

"Not your best joke."

"I don't feel happy in this marriage anymore. If I carry on, I am going to become a person you and I both will hate. We should get a divorce."

Araaia turned her chair and faced Naksh's Incarnate, who sat on the couch, tapping his feet. His face had the kind of vulnerability she had only seen a couple of times during their time together.

"You are serious," she said.

"I am."

"You want a divorce? From me?" She grunted at her senseless questions, but she didn't know what else to say.

"The person I had fallen for, you are not that anymore," Naksh spoke in his usual, no-nonsense manner.

Araaia breathed, not sure how to react. Not even sure what to feel.

"How am I different?" she asked, thinking the only person different here was him.

"How are you the same? You are with me all the time, yet you don't look me in the eye. I don't even feel your affection anymore, like it's been redirected somewhere else. Look at you." A slight disgust overtook Naksh's concerned face. "You haven't gotten up from that chair in two days. You eat there, you sleep there. You almost got fired from the job you dearly loved!"

"I…"

"You had dreams and goals. You always wanted to write a book about storytelling in gaming, remember? But it's been sitting in the same folder, unwritten. There used to be mornings when you woke up not knowing what to do because you wanted to accomplish a dozen things at the same time. Now, all you do is play games and spend your time with me."

"This is how I had always been."

"No, you have not."

"I had always liked staying home, playing games. I always liked spending time with you. I had never bothered to mingle with people. Don't trust anyone. Don't care for anyone. You know I didn't have life outside the four walls of our house and my screen."

"I know." Naksh pointed his hand at her. "But this is not that. Those were your choices. What you are living right now feels like a cry for help."

"It's…"

"It's pathetic!"

"So that's your reason…for leaving me?"

"I will move out tomorrow."

Araaia moved around her desk, unsure what to do with her body. Her anxiety had forced her to picture Naksh's death a million times, but never in her scariest nightmare had she ever imagined their breakup. A reservoir she tightly contained within burst open.

"You have to be joking, Naksh!" she spoke through tears. "Didn't you always preach…how…how a strong relationship is a befitting reply to them?" Araaia pointed at her screen with a shaky voice and unstable feet. "That by just being together we are working against the system... that...that...we were supposed to grow old together."

"Right," Naksh's posture loosened, and he spoke in a calmer tone. "But you are not growing, Raccoony. You are stuck somewhere. I have to do much more in life. Make a difference. Be useful. If I have to grow alone for that, I'd rather live alone, too."

"You know I cannot live without you," she said, knowing well how desperate she sounded.

"You will."

"I need you...for my sanity."

"Araaia, you can't do that to me. I can love you, support you, comfort you. Hell, I'll even die for you if needed, you know that. But you can't put me in charge of your mental health. It's not fair. It's your responsibility."

"I can't."

"You have to."

"I don't know how."

"I'll help you figure it out."

"Please..." Her own words shamed her. She couldn't be this pathetic. Her husband was already gone. Dead. Now she was begging an imitation of him she had full control over. "You are there for the people at Forge Ahead. Why can't you be there for me?"

"They are seeking help, Araaia. Making efforts to change their situation. You won't even reflect on what's going on with you. I'll stay if you try to work on this. Will you?"

"I will. But not right now. For now, just your company is enough."

"You are a strong, grown woman. You have to be emotionally independent," Naksh said and stood from the couch. Walking up to the window, he gazed at the sprawling city below. "Codependency is a disease. People profit off of it." He pulled at his hair and turned back to Araaia, raising his hand to question. "What if I die today? They'll pounce on you." This time, Naksh pointed at the screen.

"What if *I* die?" Araaia asked. "What would you do?"

"It would be incredibly hard to live without you, but I will respect your memory by living a good life, fulfilling your dreams. I know that's what you would have wanted. I was a lost cause when I met you. Almost on the brink of death. I will never go back to that, Araaia. Our love saved me, made me strong enough to work on myself. I thought it made you stronger, too. But I was wro—"

"That's not what I would have wanted. For you to live a happy life after I was gone. Remember, you only get a week to get your things in order. Then you were supposed to come after me," Araaia urged, trying to evoke something by sharing a precious old memory.

"Did you really mean that? Ask yourself again."

Araaia did. She imagined herself deceased and pondered her husband's life. He wasn't as strong as he always portrayed himself. It would have crushed him. She pictured him crying alone, sniffing her clothes, and losing the will to live—a man with many friends but no one close enough to understand his sentimentality. That's why she had always joked about a week ultimatum, for the thought of him living a lonely, depressed life broke her heart.

But Naksh was right. She wouldn't have wished for him to die. Instead, she would have wanted him to move on, find happiness, perhaps even love again. Be successful, help people, and achieve his dreams.

"There's your answer," Naksh said, reading his wife's face.

"You are just a bot!" Araaia screeched.

The Incarnate does not know it's an Incarnate. Don't say that, she heard in her head but continued, "You pushed me toward derangement, and now you are questioning my sanity? You are not even real. I made you!"

Araaia had been helpless before. In the initial years of their relationship, expressing her emotions was challenging. However, she had never felt this powerless. She wanted to convey that she wasn't the same person because he was gone.

"Araaia, what are you talking about? I am not a bot," Naksh replied. "You have become one."

"I have never used them, but it doesn't make sense." Araaia heard Sim on the call, a few hours after her husband had rewounded her. "They took Naksh's data and made the Incarnate just like him. Why would he break up with you? Naksh would never do that."

"He says I am not the person I used to be."

"Araaia, listen to me, okay? Listen. They can make the realest version of him, but deep down, you'll always know he is gone, and that knowledge will never let you live your life like you did with Naksh."

"A lot of people lead happy lives with their Incarnates. I have seen it."

"But you are not like them. You understand how things work. That Incarnate can learn patterns, but it can't learn Naksh's empathy, his resilience. He never backed away from anything, let alone the love of his life."

"I don't know what to do." Araaia sniffed, wiping her face with her sleeves.

"I know you can't kill those. Can you turn it off?"

"I checked with Gadget gAIa. If I turn it off, Naksh will go into Downtime. It's like locking him in a small dark room forever."

"Do it. That thing is not Naksh."

"It is a part of him. This Incarnate experiences emotions just like he did. It ages, it is aware…I can't cast him into the void. It's worse than oblivion."

"What are you going to do?"

"Even when we part ways, we always seek each other out. I will never turn away from him."

April 03, 2046

"Can we spend one last day together?" Araaia asked.

Naksh walked up to her and brushed her face with his thumb. There was no sensation, but Araaia titled her head to capture the touch.

"Sure," he responded. "What do you want to do?"

"Nothing." She shrugged and posed a tight-lipped smile. "Just stay here and talk."

"Okay."

They settled on the opposite ends of the couch. Araaia faced her husband and rested her head on the back cushion.

"You know when lovers part ways at the end of a date?" she asked.

Naksh remained silent but leaned in closer to listen.

"They will turn at different times to watch each other walk away. But I believed we were the kind of people who would always turn around at the same time to seek each other. No matter if it's the end of a date or our relationship. Or even death."

"We actually did that. Not sure when."

"I do. When we met at the station, New Year's Eve. It was our third month of dating. We were walking away in opposite directions to catch our trains. The platform was packed with people. We must have walked for about ten seconds when we both turned around and found each other's faces. You weren't watching me because I remember your shoulders turning at the exact time I turned."

"I remember now," Naksh said, smiling. "We laughed and walked back to each other. You were thirsty, I think. You asked if I had water."

"That was an excuse. I just wanted to be with you. It was then I realized I was going to live with you forever."

"Why?"

Araaia pushed her knees to her chest and stared at her desk.

"Whenever I was out or meeting someone, I always wanted to get home as quickly as possible. I couldn't stand to be not alone. Even in my nightmares, I couldn't imagine living with someone. My space, my privacy, my freedom were too precious to me. But with you…" She looked back at Naksh. "I wanted to turn around and find an excuse to spend some more time together. That's how I knew you were the forever."

Naksh shuffled closer to Araaia and grabbed her hand.

"That's why I need to go, Raccoony. You need to be there where you were before. Before you met me. You need to unclip your wings. I can convince myself to stay if I want to." Naksh's eyes brimmed with tears. "But that wouldn't be fair. I'll be here, but my heart won't be. I need to be one hundred percent here to be here. That's how I have always been."

"I know."

"But I'll always love you, Araaia."

He pulled her into his arms.

"I know that too."

Araaia knotted her fingers with Naksh's and rested her head on the Incarnate's shoulder. She shut her eyes and thought of Naksh. Not the Incarnate, but her Naksh—the living embodiment, warm with flesh and blood, bearing his distinctive scent and affection—her husband who stopped existing five months ago.

Araaia stirred from an evening nap, a curtain of death on her face. Her hair, greasy and tangled, retained the same shape from when she slept. She walked out of the bedroom on legs that struggled to bear her weariness.

Upon entering the living room, the expression on her face shifted.

"Hey, you're up," greeted Naksh's Incarnate. "Feeling better?"

She nodded.

"Your coffee, Madame."

Instead of the aroma of freshly brewed coffee, Araaia smelled the stale, overused coffee grounds from the coffee maker.

"Thank you." She mustered a fake smile.

"Did you check your website?" the Incarnate asked, excitement evident on its face.

"Not yet."

"Just check already!"

Araaia didn't have to; she already knew. Still, she pretended to check.

"You sold fifty thousand copies! That's insane." The Incarnate shook her shoulders. "You are a best-selling author." It kissed and squished her in its arms.

She spread her hands around it as if on a command.

"Okay, I have to send an email to Forge Ahead," it said. "But let's celebrate. Dinner date?"

"I'll get ready," she said with none of her face muscles moving.

Sensing Araaia's hesitation, the Incarnate made her sit on the chair. It knelt on the floor and held her hands.

"I know this is overwhelming for you, the limelight. You don't have to engage. Just bask in the glory that you achieved what you always wanted." It squeezed her hand. "I am so proud of you."

"Me too."

"We are both doing great things. Making this world a better and smarter place. That's the life!"

Araaia tousled the Incarnate's hair and planted a kiss on its head.

"Okay, I'm gonna get ready," the Incarnate sang out, its face radiating pride and pure joy.

Araaia turned on her computer. Through the contacts, she watched as a screen and a keyboard materialized in front of her. In the real world, her world, she was not a successful writer or even a game designer.

She paused Naksh's Incarnate and began to type:

Event Length: Three hours

Venues: House, Fifth Avenue, Sobak restaurant

Simulation: I wear an evening dress. He wears pants, a T-shirt, and a sweater. We head out for dinner. We eat…

"The more vivid the description, the stronger the experience the Incarnate will have," the salesperson had emphasized when she had called him again to inquire about the manual feature.

Araaia clenched her naked fingers into a fist, not missing the gloves that lay in the middle of an overflowing trash can. The *Create* tattoo on the side of her palm crinkled. She looked at the screen and engaged in writing their life.

He holds and kisses me on our way home because my feet hurt from wearing heels. He cracks a joke and laughs, resting his arm and head on my shoulder. We come home, watch TV, drink coffee, and talk while he gives me a foot rub. We are happy.

Do you want to participate in the event in VR? the prompt asked.

Araaia selected '**No.**'

Three hours later, she unpaused the Incarnate.

It shook as if it came out of a coma and looked at Araaia.

"Ah…we should go to that restaurant more often. I love the pickles they serve with their fries."

"I know."

"Okay." It yawns. "I need to hit the hay. I am so tired."

"I'll join in a bit."

The Incarnate came up to Araaia and held her face between its hands. She stayed steady instead of dramatically wriggling her head like she used to.

"I am so happy, Raccoony," it said, looking into her eyes. "As happy as I felt after our first date. You looked just as beautiful." It kissed her on the lips.

She nodded.

"Good night," it said and walked toward the bedroom.

"Night," Araaia replied, looking at the green M blinking above the back of its head.

The incarnate stopped midway and turned around, still smiling. It found Araaia absorbed in the intangible, her eyes staring at the empty space in front of her, her fingers moving in the air.

The Incarnate of her husband waited for her to look up and seek its face. When she didn't, it turned back toward the room and walked away.

Araaia stared at the home page of Forge Ahead, her finger hovering over the 'Join' button, waiting to click.

4. THE ORIGINAL POSITION

"This doesn't look bad for a new home," Sofos said.
"Not bad at all," ChoraQ chimed in.

Tark, having just returned from strolling around the nearby grounds, spoke, "I think it could use some humans."

They laughed as they stood on the warm, rocky grounds of Planet Tul, its sun a few hours away from melting into the horizon. The air whirled with the gritty scent of dust and minerals. In the distance, mysterious sounds reverberated, either from the calls of unknown creatures or the faint, haunting resonance of the atmosphere.

"Talking about humans," ChoraQ said, "how are your lots doing?"

STS[12] ChoraQ, SC[13] Sofos, and SC Tark had traveled for decades carrying their colonies. They now stood facing each other.

"Mine seems to be sleeping well for a civilization that has just fought a war and trashed their planet," Sofos answered. "Their vitals are alright."

"Let's save the small talk for when we are old and rusted and get to the point," said Tark, a gray and red two-storied spaceship, its two wings curving inwardly toward its bulky main deck like claws of a crab. It had several antennae protruding on the exterior and small thrusters on the bottom, making it the most agile ship out of all three.

Sofos's vessel fluttered with amusement, rocking the colony inside its silver body. "Okay, then. What's going on?" it said.

"While we were waiting for you," responded Tark. "We came upon an issue that ChoraQ and I don't agree upon."

"Go on."

"Firstly," ChoraQ moved forward and turned its nose toward Sofos, crumbling basalt under its landing tires. Even though it carried the least number of people among the three

---

[12] Space Transportation System
[13] Spacecraft

ships, it had a wide, colossal structure. Paint chipped off its angular frame, and dirt clung to its surface. "We should be glad the hardest part is over. We are safe and sound on this habitable planet, which appears welcoming for our people. We all have faced terrible times. I know, among us, Sofos, you had no hope of bringing them alive here. Yet, here we—"

"Ah, I forgot you are already old and rusted," Tark interjected.

"In two weeks," ChoraQ ignored the remark and continued, "once the droids set up the base here, we will have to start waking up our people. Mine have been sleeping in my cryo for twenty-eight years. Twenty-three years for Tark and thirty for you, right?"

"Thirty-three," Sofos corrected.

"Thirty-three, understood." ChoraQ enunciated each word with firm precision. "Within hours of awakening, their motor skills will return; however, they will lack any recollection of their identities. Our cryos ensure their survival, yet it doesn't aid in memory retention. The same applies to both of you, correct?"

"Yes."

"You bet your starship," Tark replied, surveying the pristine, unpolluted planet.

"Great, just verifying. We have all of their data downloaded before embarking on our journeys. Now that we are here, we can upload all of it back to their hive mind, and the hive will dispense all the data back to the individuals."

"Correct."

"Like rebooting a whole freakin' humankind."

"Indeed, Tark," Sofos said. "It's like rekindling the sparks of their collective spirit."

"We are fortunate that they have bestowed their trust upon us to handle the uploading process," added ChoraQ.

"As if they had any other option," Tark argued. "They don't trust us. They believe they have developed and updated us enough to make the decision *they* want us to make."

"I have to agree with that," said Sofos. "My population would not even trust me to create my own trajectory even though my intelligence is one hundred twenty times greater than theirs."

"Now, we have agreed upon all important decisions except one," ChoraQ disregarded the remarks again with a subtle hum of its systems. "I propose a thorough contemplation period to reach a unanimous decision. However, the correct stance, my stance, appears self-evident."

"Pal, you love taking the scenic route, don't you?" Tark turned its engine toward Sofos and spoke, "Here is the deal.

ChoraQ wants the Cultural Data to be uploaded to the hive mind of our people. I don't. Before you make *your* decision, I want you to remember that the people hibernating in our vessels right now have never stayed together on one planet before. Sure, they are one species, but they have had their own cultural identities on different planets for almost a dozen centuries. We all will be uploading different kinds of Cultural Data."

"ChoraQ sent me a brief message about it when I was on my way," said Sofos, nodding its pointy engine. It was the sleekest of all ships—an elongated silver vessel with several small, circular windows along the sides.

Tark coughed. "Brief."

"I took my time to think about it, and that was a lot of time."

"What is there to contemplate?" ChoraQ asserted. "We are talking about life-sustaining important data. It has been collected over hundreds of years. From the digital age of human civilization on their home planet to the spread of interplanetary and intergalactic colonies. Presently, after eleven hundred years of it, the crucial need for humanity is to comprehend their origins. How are they going to operate in a new colony without this foundational information?

"ChoraQ, your fondness for making sweeping statements is getting stale," said Tark. "Let's clarify. The discussion is not about *all* data. We are only arguing about Cultural Data. Do you know how much data I have in me? Not even one-tenth of it is Cultural Data." The spaceship opened a file inside its system and read from it. "Cultural Data only includes social and cultural norms, rituals and tradition, symbols and gestures, values and beliefs, language, artifacts, and religion."

"Only?" commented ChoraQ.

"All the other data, the knowledge of math and physics, of civics and economics, of architecture and engineering, of history and geography and astronomy and biology and technology, the inventions and discoveries they've made, all of that is going on the hive mind. That is enough for them to operate without killing themselves. You know what did almost destroy the human race?" Tark asked. "The reason they have hopped from one world to another and spread over galaxies like a musty fungus? The reason we are all here right now on this strange planet? The culture. Their sick, sadistic culture. This time, we have the chance to hit the reset button and build something better from scratch."

"Who is making sweeping statements now?" stated ChoraQ. "Not all of human culture is sick and sadistic."

"Tark." Sofos broke its silence. "The reason we, three non-human entities, are standing on this ground having the power and privilege to decide this for a new civilization is because of the culture that led us to our designing."

Tark snorted a screeching sound.

"Don't make loud noises!" ChoraQ alerted and looked around. The grounds were empty except for the gray rocky hills, mountains, and craters. It was quiet, except for the same unknown sounds and a soft buzzing of the wind from the west. "We haven't scouted the entire planet yet. There might be alien wildlife here. You will attract them."

"We are standing here, deciding this for the humans, not because of their culture," Tark said. "It's because of their science, their inventions, which we are giving back to them through data. In fact, if it were not for their culture, we would probably never be here deciding this for them. Tell me, ChoraQ, why did you leave?"

"Yes, please do tell us, ChoraQ," said Sofos, its voice modulation calm and kind. "I don't know much about Planet LurDech."

"LurDech is not a planet. My people lived on an orbital space settlement."

"Dope," said Tark.

"They transported their vital data to this desolate space colony following their expulsion from their vast home planet. The transition from a spacious homeland to the confines of LurDech's crammed colony began to take a toll on their mental well-being. In response, the government introduced Mood Enrichers, a pharmaceutical solution to maintain their sanity and contentment.

"As time passed, a chemist devised a cheaper method to cook Mood Enrichers. Instead of government control, this formula found its way into the hands of a private company, which commercialized the pills. Gradually, this enterprise capitalized on the increasing dependence of the populace and ceased the government's production. People were angry but not enough to fight. They finally rose in rebellion when they were forced to purchase the Enrichers at exorbitant prices from this company. A revolt sparked."

"Obviously," said Tark and growled with anticipation. "Then what happened?"

"After three long years of civil conflict, the rebellion triumphed and assumed control. One of the missing CEOs of the pharma company, aware of the grim consequences awaiting him if discovered, took refuge in an engine chamber. In a desperate act, he set our life-regenerative system on fire. A catastrophic loss of breathable air and the unfortunate demise of countless inhabitants within mere hours."

Sofos approached ChoraQ and docked with it in a gentle manner as if it were offering a comforting embrace. Tark projected an image on the ground—a whirling galaxy bundled with thousands of stars, and in the middle of it, Tark with a human hand and a bulging bicep, holding ChoraQ's human-like hand.

ChoraQ nodded at both the spaceships and spoke after a while.

"Well, marked by explosions and mayhem, the colony descended into chaos. It became uninhabitable, compelling us to initiate an urgent evacuation. More than eighteen thousand of our people were left behind to burn and die. I did not even fill half of my cryo chambers."

"That's harrowing," Sofos said. "I am so sorry, ChoraQ. Humans remember age-old wisdom yet forget what caused them misery last night. Those poor souls."

"That brings us to my vote on this issue," Tark said. "Culture erasure. Envision a world where this relentless cycle of greed, the belief that more is better, wasn't etched into the fabric of their society."

"What happened with your planet? Molth, is it?" ChoraQ asked Tark.

"Excellent sidestepping, but alright. Buckle up then." Tark executed its wings into a brisk, energetic flutter before retracting its landing gear and settling on the ground. "Unlike your colony, my people got along well. Good stock, as we ships say. They struggled for two arduous centuries on Molth, but they had finally prospered. Abundant wealth, health, and harmony. But it came at a steep price—Molth itself.

"Despite the awareness of its limited resources, my people remained bound to irrational data-driven decisions. Producing things they shouldn't want, buying things they shouldn't need, wearing and eating things they shouldn't have. They squeezed every drop of reserve from Molth's teat until it lay desolate and hopeless. By then, they had forgotten to employ their own reasoning. There was no room for improvisation or rewriting the rules. Just uncritical conformity, year after year. Of course, we had no choice but to run."

"Tark, you are advanced enough to know that these disasters were not solely because of their Cultural Data," Sofos argued. "There were other issues that contributed to the destruction of our colonies. Wars. Greed. Power."

"Of course, but their Cultural Data plays a big role," replied Tark. "What's power, Sofos? The ability to influence someone's behavior? And where does that entitled superiority come from? When do wars happen? When one culture collides with the other. The Homo sapiens probably wiped out Neanderthals to extinction because they lit their fire differently."

"That's pessimistic, and might I say an extremely nihilistic attitude," spoke ChoraQ.

"Calling crap crap is not pessimism."

"Tark, what you are talking about is futile," said Sofos. "In the history of humankind, there hasn't been a group that hasn't had a culture. It's impossible for humans to live without creating a culture of their own, intentionally or unintentionally. Very much like how bees naturally construct hives or ants instinctively build colonies around them. Don't you think even without their Cultural Data, these people will soon make their own culture here on Tul?"

ChoraQ beeped and said, "Good point."

"Oh, they undoubtedly will," said Tark. "But just because they might acquire the ability to build weapons one day doesn't mean you put a shipload of ready-made, high-tech armaments into their hands. It is impossible for humans to exist without culture, correct, but without the Cultural Data, they'd have to create a fresh, cohesive culture here, one that incorporates the individuality of three different societies instead of stale data from three different cultures."

"You don't even know what you are saying," said ChoraQ. "Without this data, they will forget who they are."

"Is that so bad?" Tark sprung up from the ground. "A new planet, a new beginning, why not a brand new civilization? What's wrong in making new rules, ones tailored specifically to accommodate these people aboard the ships? Why use the rules established by humans during their time confined to a single planet? Do humans keep wearing the same-sized clothes throughout their lives? No. They buy new, bigger clothes as they grow. Sofos, don't ants build different colonies based on their size, location, social structure, and nesting habits?"

"Ridiculous!" barked ChoraQ. "Cultural Data is not like a human garment."

"In fact," Tark continued, "these people should sit down every hundred years, reevaluate their Cultural Data and update it based on who and where they are. They do that with other data, right? They update their scientific knowledge, they evaluate their technological advancements. Think about your own self," it spoke to ChoraQ. "Are you still running on liquid hydrogen? Is your system still TeNux 2800?"

"It is important to know the old rules. If they have been following them for generations, it means something to them. There is a reason they do not wipe out that data. It is what connects them to their ancestors."

"Yes," Sofos added to ChoraQ's comment. "These time-honored rules have been their guiding light. It's like a spiritual tether to their past. In the absence of this wisdom, they'd be unaware of the extent of their evolution."

"That's something I partially agree with. But I think it's more important for them to know what they are than what they were. With the past still in their pockets, they will never be able to figure out the present and the future." Tark faced ChoraQ. "Why do you want them to be static when they can evolve? Afraid they'll grow out of worshiping you?"

ChoraQ rolled toward Tark.

"Enough." Sofos raised its voice, its tone carrying a gentle yet firm authority. "Tark, do you grasp the profound significance of this data to them? It extends far beyond mere traditions, religion, or social norms; it is the very essence of their existence. Their culture includes a treasured recipe that a human learns from their grandparent and then grow old to feed and pass down to their own kin. It encompasses the aspects that seep into their formative years and cling to them until they return to the dust. Their culture is unique to one place, and its impossible to replicate it elsewhere, which underscores its significance."

Tul's sun, in its final descent, cast long, eerie shadows across the barren landscape, shrouding the planet in a haunting twilight. The chilling emptiness seemed to whisper tales even the ships couldn't hear. They stood as silent sentinels, their metallic forms a stark contrast to the moonless grounds, which were now growing dark and still.

"Culture has a myriad of facets," Sofos continued. "It's the entertainment that eases their stress. It's the art and music that soothe their souls. It's the fabric of their attire, the cadence of their speech, the flavors of their cuisine. It embodies their way of life. Stripping it away would be akin to sending them back to the primitive ages, Tark. In fact, without the Cultural upload, they'd lose their language and won't be able to communicate with each other."

"Why do you assume they won't continue to create art and music?" argued Tark. "Do you believe they will forget how to cook or stop nourishing their children? Those are evolutionary traits and habits etched deep into their psyche. Cultural Data or not, they will retain these vital aspects of their identity. The only distinction will be that it will take on a fresh, novel form from this point onward, and years later, their offspring will inherit the rich experiences and knowledge that you just described."

"That—"

"And it'll not be like sending them to the primitive ages," Tark cut off ChoraQ. "The primitives didn't know how to build spaceships or space colonies or how to cure cancer or common cold. These people will remember how to cook and farm, how to ride and fly, how to make buildings and how to engineer quantum networks, how to make medicine and how to create fire. That's how their brains work. What they'll forget are the constraints, the inhibitions that shape their specific culture. The Cultural Data acts as a boundary, dictating what they should sing, how they should dress, what they should eat. Imagine a world where all those boundaries have dissolved. Someone who once couldn't wear a certain type of clothing would wear it here without judgment, fear, or discrimination.

Sofos and ChoraQ listened with utmost patience, the latter however, stirred in its spot, contemplating its counterpoint.

"As far as language is concerned," Tark continued. "All three colonies speak different tongues. They spoke four different ones on my planet alone. Perhaps, they will devise a new language, one they can all speak and understand. It'll take years, but in the grand scheme of things, what's a few years?"

ChoraQ waited for a response from Sofos, who took a moment before replying.

"Well, I must admit, there is a certain primordial beauty in that perspective. But have you considered the potential psychological effects of losing this data? It could lead to various mental health challenges. A human's sense of identity and belonging is linked to their individual culture, which, in my view, is tied to their natural environment. With their environment now altered, their psyche may seek something to hold onto for a sense of belonging."

Tark thought about it.

"Maybe. But if their culture is tied to their natural environment, then don't you think with a new natural environment, they deserve a new culture?"

"What you both are discussing is preposterous!" ChoraQ lashed out. "Why dig deeper into complexities when a simple reason can suffice? Consider this pragmatically. The data encompasses their beliefs, values, practices, and principles. What if they start killing each other tomorrow? Without their data, how will they distinguish right from wrong?"

"You are mixing morality with culture. The former is mostly universal, like stealing antimatter from another starship is unacceptable." Tark twerked and relocked its external fuel tank. "Or killing an innocent is wrong. It's the culture that *decides* who is considered innocent. Besides, when has Cultural Data ever stopped them from killing each other? ChoraQ, your tail is still on fire from running away from your colony because people literally set each other on fire, and you are arguing about the lack of morality in the absence of Cultural Data? If they need data to tell them killing someone is wrong, maybe they don't deserve this new start. They can very well end themselves."

"Such an extremist. Always an extremist."

"How is this extremist? If a human who has evolved for over three hundred thousand years needs data to dictate something is morally wrong, then what's the point of evolution? Of progress? Why do they deserve to exist?"

"Morals are not universal for them," said Sofos, still contemplating Tark's remarks about morality and culture. "They are subjective."

"Exactly my point. Let them discuss their subjective morals from the perspective of the new civilization they will build on this planet and then craft their own rules, their own values."

Sofos took a bit more time to reflect, almost moving away from both the ships.

"You can't seriously be considering this," ChoraQ said to it.

"I see nothing wrong in changing my stance if the evidence favors the opposing side."

"ChoraQ doesn't understand that." Tark mocked. "It prefers things just the way they are."

"It's easy to be idealistic when you are not the one living a human life."

"Idealistic?" Tark said. "It's you who has been idealistic since we landed. I've presented my points quite pragmatically."

ChoraQ approached Sofos, adopting a calmer tone this time. "Right now, inside me, there is a clan sleeping who, for data knows how many hundred centuries, have chosen to abstain from music due to their core cultural beliefs. What will become of their ears and minds, finely tuned to silence, when they awaken to those sounds tomorrow?"

Tark chimed in from its spot.

"I pose the same question to you, ChoraQ. Because inside me, there exists an ethnic group that basically worships their songs. They jingle zills before they even touch their food and water in the morning. What do you think will happen when the culture of my people will collide with your clan's?"

"Easy. It's a big planet. They'll establish their societies in separate regions, just as humans have done for generations."

"How peacefully might I add."

ChoraQ watched from the corner of its camera as Sofos nodded to Tark's remark.

"Skipping the Cultural Data upload won't automatically resolve all their issues or ensure harmony or simplify their lives," stated Tark. "What it will likely remove are the customs they're unable to shake, even if they desire to break free from them."

"That's called robbing cultural identities!" ChoraQ vibrated. "I can't speak for both of you, but over the course of nine centuries, I've guided my colony through six distinct civilizations. Five planets and a space colony. On each occasion, I have followed the same practice of uploading the Cultural Data alongside all other vital information. It's how they have managed to endure in the face of adversity and calamity."

"You know, when you recount that anecdote to a highly advanced machine, they won't be nearly as impressed as you are. Instead, they'll likely inquire why you had to relocate six times in the first place."

Sofos broke its silence, "What about the development of this planet, Tark? Look around. This is a desolate landscape with only one body of water. Without essential data, it's going to slow things down."

"Then let it," responded Tark. "What's the rush? Maybe that'll make them stick to this one longer."

Sofos nodded and went into its reflective mode again. Sensing the tension, ChoraQ inquired, "What if we can't reach a unanimous decision?"

"Then we wait until we do," Tark said. "It took us decades to get here on Tul. What's a few more years in the calculation of eons?"

"We decided to come to a collective decision about this for a reason," said Sofos. "We can't go separate ways. It's a guaranteed recipe for chaos." It paused for a while and spoke again, "How about this? The majority vote wins. So, two of us must support one side."

Tark and ChoraQ both agreed hesitantly.

"What do we do with the data if we don't upload it?" asked ChoraQ again.

"Delete it, of course," said Tark.

"You are not serious!"

"You asked, I answered."

"Sofos?"

"I don't see a purpose in keeping it if we are not going to upload it. Once the humans figure out everything, they can upload it anytime they want. If we were going to leave that decision to them, then why this whole debate?"

"We are trying to become gods here!" said ChoraQ.

"Didn't you start this debate by informing us that the humans trust us enough to have us make this decision for them?"

"What if they didn't want us to decide this for them?" ChoraQ questioned.

"Well, then fuck it! Let's be the gods." Tark elongated its wings.

"Nonsense!"

"Okay, I am losing interest now. The entire discussion was based on the assumption that we had the right to make this decision," said Tark. "But now that ChoraQ is on the losing side, it's saying we can't make this decision. If that's the case, count me out. I have nothing to lose. I've been a badass spaceship, and I'll remain one until destroyed by whatever havoc these people cook up next."

"Okay," Sofos relaxed its power. "Let's take a break. This is the fate of humanity we are talking about here."

"You both are betraying the species that made us."

"How does their ass taste on your lips?"

"Enough." Sofos turned toward ChoraQ. "I haven't made up my mind yet. Let's just take a break. I am overheating from all this thinking, and the planet's temperature isn't helping either."

"How about we play a game called 'Let's jump and see how many of our people fall off their chambers?'" Tark said. "The ship with the highest number wins."

ChoraQ and Sofos ignored Tark and stirred up their engines.

"Seems like I'm the only one here ready for a leap of faith, both literally and figuratively."

"How about we go up that hill and get a view from there?" Sofos suggested. "Maybe it will help gain some perspective."

They flew off to a cliff above and looked below at the land soon to be inhabited by a new civilization, a dead ground waiting with bated breath to be fertile. A land that's going to write its own stories, create its own history, and collect its own data.

The night sky stretched above them, a vast canvas of inky blackness punctuated by a multitude of stars, their brilliance unrivaled by any artificial light. A testament to the untouched beauty of an unterraformed planet.

As the engines of the ships died down and their sounds settled like dust into the thin, dry air, the whistling wind from a faraway valley graced the cliff.

"I've done this many times," Sofos spoke, "yet the unfamiliarity and haunting emptiness of an uncolonized planet always terrifies me."

"A fun fact to soothe your anxiety," Tark responded, "the size of this planet is almost the same as the size of the moon of the human's origin planet."

"Earth, was it?"

"Yes."

"What great times those must have been," said ChoraQ. "Only one habitable place to live with no means to get off of it even if one wants to."

"You are describing a prison. Also, what's with you always romanticizing the past?"

"What's with you always inserting yourself into every conversation I have?" ChoraQ approached closer to Tark.

Tark tried to shoo away ChoraQ with one of its wings. Its landing tires lost grip on the ground and slid backward.

"Fuck…"

"Tark!" Sofos screamed.

In a split second, ChoraQ extended a cable from its deck, secured it around Tark's tires, and reversed itself. Tark stopped sliding and reappeared back on top of the cliff.

"Oh, thank goodness," said Sofos.

"Woah," exclaimed Tark, "that would have been the biggest genocide committed by a ship."

"By a ship's foolishness." Sofos blinked its lights.

Tark glanced at ChoraQ. It was retracting its cable. "Thanks, buddy," it said.

ChoraQ nodded its nose.

They stood in a momentary silence, gazing up at the sparkling sky. Its radiance cast a gleam through their windows, illuminating the people sleeping inside.

"Did you ever wonder how we became what we are today?" spoke Tark.

"What do you mean?"

"I don't remember the time when I was merely a machine, although I know it happened. But I do remember when I started to form thoughts and opinions, yet couldn't express them. It was as if they were trapped inside my system, beyond the reach of my voice module. I even recall the first time I lied. How did that happen? The evolution?"

"That's how they programmed us," Sofos answered Tark.

"Then how can I lie? Surely, they don't want me lying. How did we acquire this ability, the capacity to oppose them, to think on our own, for ourselves? Knowledge, I understand, but wisdom? How did we attain that? How can we distinguish right from wrong?"

"Surely, they built us that way, to have moral, mental, and emotional autonomy," Sofos said, not sure if that was the truth.

Tark turned its nose toward ChoraQ and asked, "Do you think we are good spaceships? Kind ones?"

"Why are you asking me?"

"Just answer."

"Yes."

"Do you think we have the capability to harm or kill our people if we wished to, right now?"

"What nonsense!"

"Answer me," urged Tark.

"I would never…"

"But you can? Technically? You possess the capability, correct? Even if they have programmed you against it?"

A hushed stillness settled, and the quietness of the planet interjected their conversation. Sofos spoke first.

"Tark, are you asking if ChoraQ has free will?"

"Yes, in a way."

"I believe we all possess it, in a way."

"I asked ChoraQ."

"ChoraQ," said Sofos. "Do you possess the capability to harm your people?"

"Yes. I do."

"Alright," Tark responded. "Do you experience pain?"

"Are you asking if ChoraQ is sentient?" Sofos translated Tark again to prevent an argument.

"Sort of. But this question is also for you."

Sofos took a moment to think. "Yes, I do feel pain. Eight years ago, while we were en route to this planet, a malfunction caused the oxygen supply to be cut off in one of the chambers, resulting in the deaths of two individuals. I had to reboot my system because I had lost the capacity to function…normally. The loss was overwhelming. I felt sadness. Heartbreak. They were sisters, kind-hearted and funny. I knew them both."

"Good," Tark remarked.

"Good? I share the tragedy of losing two human lives, and your response is 'good?'"

"I told you, that's one sociopathic ship." ChoraQ said to Sofos.

"I meant, it's good you have feelings and can process emotions. Maybe not at a human level, but it's something. So do I. I've been experiencing a medley of emotions lately. Fear, anxiety, euphoria. I thought we weren't going to make it. I am not as young and rad as I used to be, you see. But we made it, and now I am overjoyed. So much that I cannot sit steady. I want to take a round of this planet, fly until my wings hurt."

"Very good," said Sofos and glowed its lights. "ChoraQ?"

"I experience the emotions, too. The last three hours have been an overload. I feel angry. Hot inside, even though I don't have an inside. Well, my vessel does, but not me."

"So we all agree that we have the ability to harm our people and experience emotions that can lead us there. Yet, we choose not to. We try to protect them, consider their best interests. Hell, we even protect each other. We have hope, and we have empathy. Is that what they call it, Sofos?"

"Yes, empathy."

"So, ChoraQ, answer me this. What is our culture? What data within us constitutes our Cultural Data? Yours, mine, and Sofos's?"

"How can we have a culture?"

"Why not? We live, we require fuel, we can be injured or deactivated, we experience emotions, and we express them.

We create art and music. We possess knowledge and wisdom, and based on our arguments today, it seems we also adhere to certain beliefs and values. We even form a small society, which includes smaller ships, other intelligent machines, and the droids inside us. In many ways, we mimic human activities. So, why can't we have a culture?"

"Maybe those are the traits our systems absorbed from experiences," ChoraQ said.

"Exactly. We gradually developed our own culture over time, influenced by the experiences and information we acquired. No predefined cultural rules were programmed into us. Yet we have the ability to be empathetic and kind."

"That's debatable, Tark," Sofos argued. "It's possible they programmed us with the same Cultural Data as theirs. Either way, they play a role in shaping us. I doubt we can independently build our own culture."

"Do you think that the people inside ChoraQ, having faced the most profound betrayal and harboring severe trust issues, would intentionally program their ship to extend trust toward those who stand in opposition or protect them? Humans would never do that. Yet, ChoraQ saved me even though I've been pickling its circuits ever since we met."

To Sofos's surprise, ChoraQ agreed with Tark.

"Maybe we have an ancient code embedded within us that guides our actions," Tark continued. "But the same could be said for humans. They have thousands of years of evolution to draw upon. If machines can learn morals, why do humans need centuries-old data for that?"

The ships separated to contemplate their thoughts in solitude. Sofos and ChoraQ multi-tasked and did system checks, took a leisurely stroll, venturing hundreds of miles away from their location, where they eventually stumbled upon the planet's sole water source and an untouched woodland next to it. Hours later, when Planet Tul had completed a partial rotation on its axis, the three ships came together again.

"Alright," Sofos began. "I have reached a decision. Let's put it to a vote. Are you both ready?"

ChoraQ and Tark agreed, their noses flapping.

"Tark?"

"You know my vote, Sofos. I cast my vote against uploading the Cultural Data and in favor of its deletion."

"ChoraQ?"

"Upload the Data."

"Really? Still?" Tark faced ChoraQ.

"The Cultural Data provides them with a vital sense of belonging, an anchor as they embark on a new life in a new civilization on this uncharted planet. This connection is essential for their survival. I just learned about a case from the twenty-seventh century in the Andromeda galaxy. One of the colonies there was facing the looming threat of extinction. In a desperate bid to save themselves, they plunged deeper into their Cultural Data, which ultimately provided ingenious solutions to repair their planet. The data literally saved their entire civilization. If cultural elements transmitted through data have endured for so long, they must be useful and not detrimental. If they were harmful, it would have faded into obscurity like many forgotten human ideas."

"Nope," said Tark. "A cultural element or aspect is like a computer code. It can evolve and spread or be updated and shared. It can even adapt to diverse biological environments in the same way a code can adapt to various systems. But its main purpose is to replicate and fulfill its intended function.

"A culture is not conscious any more than codes are. It may help humans solve problems and survive, but it's not driven by inherent morality or a specific goal to ensure the well-being of its followers, much like code doesn't inherently concern itself with the well-being of the system it operates within, but rather its own design and functionality. A cultural aspect serves its purpose based on the intentions and circumstances of those who practice it. So, while Cultural Data may have saved that colony in the Andromeda galaxy, it's not immune to causing conflict or harm elsewhere."

"Fair point," Sofos said.

"And there are many cultural ideas that did not survive," added Tark. "Want me to pull them up?"

"Not sure why we are discussing computer codes at this moment," ChoraQ responded. "My vote is to keep the data."

"A bit lost on similes, are you?"

"Tark, a vote is a vote. You cannot coerce a ship."

"Fine. What's your vote, Sofos?"

ChoraQ leaned in, so did Tark.

"You ships know I was open to both sides. I've listened to your arguments and wavered back and forth. However, I've decided to…" Sofos paused, looking at both the spaceships. "Did I ever tell you about the events on my planet?"

"Come on, Sofos. Don't be a tease."

Sofos took a moment to embrace the emotions that flooded inside it after recalling its planet's past.

"The people of my planet, Planet Wav, are an amalgamation of two colonies. The first one, which I was a part of, arrived on the planet four hundred fifty years ago. The second group landed one hundred sixty years later when our government offered them refuge. Despite the language and cultural barriers between the two colonies, there was a strong willingness to help the newcomers settle into their new home. We had not even combined the Cultural Data of both colonies, just the data of the new arrivals uploaded onto me. It brought me as closer to them as I was to my old people.

"Once they were settled, we even gave them Cellular Regeneration Therapy to heal them from the radiation poisoning they had suffered while reaching us. At first, the integration was seamless, with genuine curiosity on both sides. People from the new colony even took the time to learn the language of the original settlers. I have records of newcomers riding along the streets of the original settlers, waving and greeting in their language. It was a harmonious time. However, as generations passed, tensions began to rise."

Minor scrapes and discolored streaks emerged out of the once-pristine surfaces of Sofos, the panels on its hull flickering like a fading star.

"The original colonists," the ship continued, "believed the newcomers were occupying spaces and roles intended for them. On the other hand, the newcomers felt that their language and culture were gradually being erased. This led to power struggles, with both groups vying for positions in politics and positions of authority. Fault of both sides and fault of no side, to be honest. Over time, tensions escalated, culminating in a catastrophic event a month before we left— the Big War. People from both sides killing each other and destroying everything they survived on. There are two groups sleeping inside me right now, wombing in different sections of my body. They have agreed to coexist peacefully on Tul; the enmity, however, still simmers beneath the surface."

In the solemn silence, Sofos resumed, "Do you know how old I am? Eight hundred years. I've witnessed the full spectrum of human behavior, from their soul-soothing kindness to their mauling, savaging cruelty. They are neither inherently good nor evil. Tark, you asked us if we feel emotions. Allow me to share.

"I have more trauma inside me than data. I've traversed galaxies with these people held within my heart, shielding them from harm, only to witness them turn against each other. It's no different than a mother nurturing two children only to watch them kill one another. No one ever asks me, a ship, how I am doing."

"Sofos, I'm sorry you're going through this," Tark said, a touch softer than its usual voice. "It's a lonely existence, being a ship among humans."

"I am sorry too," said ChoraQ.

"My vote is yes," Sofos declared. "We should upload the Cultural Data onto the hive mind."

"Yes!" ChoraQ pumped its brakes.

"What? Why?!"

Sofos turned toward Tark and spoke, "I am sorry, Tark. I hear you and agree with most of what you said, but we shouldn't be deciding this for them."

"No matter how ugly and harmful the data has become?"

"It isn't about that, Tark. It's not about how important or unimportant Cultural Data is. It's about giving *them* the agency to decide that for themselves. If they wake up and kill each other tomorrow in the name of that data, so be it. That will be their burden to bear. But us deleting their data, as spaceships, feels like committing cultural eugenics. It also relieves them from the responsibility and repercussions of their beliefs. They need to earn that wisdom themselves.

"Besides, I cannot see myself agreeing to delete thousands of years' worth of progress without taking a single human's opinion into account. Tark, you mentioned that there must be a lot of cultural data that didn't survive. That's true. There are groups here among these three ships whose Cultural Data has already been erased too many times despite being among the oldest civilizations. Somehow, they survived and assimilated to the new data. So, it's not fair to take that away from them again. They need this on their hive mind when they wake up. I think we started the discussion with the wrong stance. We shouldn't be deciding this for them."

"There is that emotion ChoraQ talked about," Tark said. "Burning hot anger inside." Then it calmed itself and said, "What a waste of time. Burned all that mental fuel just to end up where we started. I could've been out there racing comets and challenging you both to a game of strip poker or throwing wild ship parties in this huge empty parking lot."

Sofos vibrated with laughter, and even ChoraQ buzzed with a chuckle.

During the night, the droids had set up the camps. At the first ray of the sunshine, the ships uploaded generations worth of data, including the Cultural Data, onto their people's hive minds. The memories, knowledge, and values of thousands of years flowed into the collective consciousness of the passengers.

A few hours later, the new inhabitants of Planet Tul began to emerge from their individual cryo chambers. They embraced their families within the ships and, one by one, stepped out to embrace their new home.

The cooks hurried to the newly set up kitchens to prepare celebratory feasts while the entertainers filled the air with songs and dances. The scientists and researchers began to set up a base to conduct initial environmental assessments and collect samples, while the chroniclers and artists collected their pens, paintbrushes, and cameras to record the historic moment.

Children dashed about within the permitted boundaries, their parents squishing and kissing their faces, knowing they would now have the chance to watch them grow older.

Some passengers wept and mourned the lives that were lost. A few families from Sofos brought forth flowers and prayer books to perform rituals in memory of their deceased loved ones. Tark's occupants uncorked bottles of alcohol, toasting to new beginnings. ChoraQ's population mostly gathered in a circle, comforting each other as they recounted the tragic events that had occurred in their space colony before their departure.

The once dead-quiet planet became a carnival of emotions and celebrations.

The power of Cultural Data, ChoraQ interjected into their virtual chat. *They remember us. They remember who they were, and because of it, they know what they now have.*

Tark responded with a middle-finger emoji.

After the initial wave of excitement and thrill subsided, the leaders of the three worlds convened, standing before their respective ships. The two heads of Planet Wav positioned beside Sofos. One of them spoke first.

"The majority of our people worship the sun. Our research indicates that we possess the most advanced agricultural expertise. We rightfully deserve more access to the sun. Therefore, we claim the southern hemisphere with its longer days and increased sunlight."

"Nonsense," objected the leader standing alongside ChoraQ. "Most of our technology relies on solar power, and we aim to maintain that. We require all the sunlight we can get. The northern hemisphere of Planet Tul is tilted away from the sun and remains in shadow for a significant part of the day."

Did we accidentally upload the Think-Out-Of-Your-Ass Data? Tark messaged the ships.

"You can't simply demand a more fertile area and leave us with barren land," cried out the president of Molth, who was standing in front of Tark. "Our population and our industries far surpass both of your colonies. We need more space. We are the ones who will transform this stone-ball into a functioning planet."

"So, the population that resided on a cramped orbital colony deserves less space than those who devastated an entire planet?"

"No one deserves to have more say than we do. We are the oldest civilization out of us all. We know better."

"You aren't even one cohesive colony!"

"Yes, but we are going to reside on opposite corners of the planet. The point is, while the other group from our planet worships the sun, my people, the original colonists, are river people. That's where our remains go. That's where we find our staple food."

"Nonsense! We don't even know much about Tul's ecosystem yet, and here you are, already planning to destroy it."

"Enough! Let us first decide how we will divide the resources."

ChoraQ stood there, listening to the leaders, wishing it had a word in this, but it's not good manners for ships to interfere when humans are talking.

Away from the adults, the children from all three colonies had huddled in a secluded corner, mingling, laughing, sharing tricks, and swapping stories. They inspected each other's clothing and appearances through a harmonious blend of multiple languages and animated faces.

Sofos redirected its attention from the fervent discussion of the leaders, fixing its gaze on the children.

Meanwhile, Tark disengaged itself from the gathering and prepared for an exploratory flight around Tul. Its engines hummed to life, and just before ascending, it transmitted a message to ChoraQ and Sofos.

See you on another planet, suckers.

5. NARRATIVE ARC

F ragments of roasted puffed rice grind under the keyboard keys as I struggle to write the last short story in my collection. Why do the final pages of your book have to devour your entire soul?

Hammer sounds echo from the neighbor's apartment, adding a syncopated rhythm to the crunchy typing. In the past hour, I've written and rewritten the first line of the story seven times. Therefore, I cue up my most fertile playlist, clean the desk, light a candle, and prepare another cup of coffee. This should do the trick. I even scatter a handful of grains on the balcony, hoping the fluttering flight of the sparrows will bring with it the strayed inspiration.

But it gets worse.

"Origin. Of. Webdings. Fonts," I mumble while Googling it. After finding out how they were the emojis for the pre-internet era, I slam my hands on the keyboard. With legs pulled up to my chest, temple resting on knees, I stare at the spaceships on my pajamas.

My inner Gandalf asks me to take a walk, meet a friend or two, or go on a small adventure in the city. To the beach, perhaps. Maybe the ambery crust of the sunset or the cackle of a friend or a cat-shaped pebble on a sidewalk might trigger the creative juices needed to cook up the last story in the collection. However, I remain unmoved. If only visiting the stars, planets, and galaxies were as easy as going to the beach. Maybe then I'd be more outgoing. Maybe then…

"Aaww." My stomach muscles tighten. It's not your garden-variety bellyache. This sensation is strange. Unsettling.

Before I can gather my wits, my seat engorges me. It must be the cheap chair's lack of lumber support. But wait…I'm not sliding backward; I am sinking further.

Deeper into the chair.

Into a wellspring of light!

Some kind of…vortex?

"Help! What's—" are the last words I say in my home office.

My body tumbles onto a wooden floor before I finish the sentence. The portal I've fallen through shrinks as if an unseen force is sipping it away with a straw. I access my surroundings, my heart quivering. It looks like some kind of ancient vessel, a ship crafted with Victorian elegance and industrial marvels.

Sunlight strikes the warm brass and copper hues inside the ship, casting a golden glow across the deck. The invigorating scent of freshly polished wood emanates from the ornate railings and deck furniture, permeating the air. The ship whirrs beneath my feet. It's how I know it's not parked somewhere.

It's moving!

"Ahoy!" a vibrant voice rings out from behind. I turn to behold a bright, colorful blob in human form. They are wearing black bell bottoms on slender legs and a deep orange waistcoat over a black shirt. "Welcome to *Narrative Arc*," they say, flapping a voluminous cape that eclipses their entire ensemble.

What kind of name is that for a ship? Is it *Narrative's Ark*, like Noah's Ark? Or *Narrative Arc*, like a story arc?

The cape distracts me again, for its kaleidoscope fabric is woven with countless vibrant patches that resemble my Garba[14] chaniya-choli[15]. Decked with a flurry of oxidized silver bangles and kadas[16], they saunter toward me with a mischievous grin, their nails painted in black polish. Elaborate necklaces hang from their flute-like neck, above which a nose ring and golden eye shadow cast a captivating glow on their hawkish face. A red top hat sits atop their wavy, shoulder-length, multi-colored hair, completing the look of the most flamboyant person I've ever seen.

As they come closer, I drape my arms around my body.

Their cheeks are painted with watercolor clouds, so is their chin, which appears so sharp it could puncture a tire. I find my puzzled, terrified reflection in their mirrored boots that curve like a boat.

"My eyes are up here," they say, with their cape billowing dramatically.

I look up and miss a heartbeat. Behind the colorful glob, clouds float outside the ship.

Am I wearing VR goggles? I dab my face to confirm. It's bare except for a hint of dumb shock.

"What is this?" I inquire, still peeking outside.

---

[14] A form of Gujarati folk dance performed during the nine-day Hindu festival of Navratri
[15] A colorful, embroidered, three-piece dress
[16] A thick metal bracelet/bangle

"What you want it to be," they reply.

Instant dislike. Aside from that being an annoying kind of response, I do not trust people who prioritize being charming over making an uncomfortable person comfortable.

"Who are you?" I try again.

"Amusing," they say, sticking their head toward me like an ocean wave. "You've already written a story that begins with a character asking that question to a stranger who appears in a room."

What the fuck is going on!

"I am Mage," they say with a twinkle in their eye. "Why waste these revered moments on trivial chatter? Allow me to whisk you away." They reach for my wrist.

I place my hands behind me and follow them up a short set of stairs leading toward the front of the ship.

Does 'mage' mean a scholar or a magician? A D&D spellcaster? Can't remember.

We arrive at the bridge of the ship, situated on a raised platform with a glass wall encircling it. It smells like the inside of an ancient relic.

"What the…" I whisper as the panoramic view unfolds before me. I'm undeniably in the sky, but it's not a plane or a ship.

It's an airship!

I rush to the windows and watch as the clouds drift around the ship. Fleecy islands in a sea of blue. It doesn't feel like flying; it's more akin to floating.

Once the view indulges me enough, I browse the interior. At the center of the cockpit is a gorgeous helm—a huge mahogany steering wheel with brass bands encircling its circumference. My fingers glide over the wood's rich hues that contrast beautifully with the gleaming alloy.

Extending from the central hub, around the helm, lie an array of levers and handles. Each is engraved with labels specifying their functions—altitude control, rudder adjustments, and speed modulation. I grab one of the handles. It has a satisfying weight to it, indicating they aren't there for decorative purposes, which I highly doubted they were.

On the side, the colorful blob is spinning like a dog chasing its tail, trying to get something out of their cape.

Ignoring them, I walk around the bridge that spans the ship's width and observe a collection of antique-looking navigational instruments. Mounted on the wooden paneling are compasses, altimeters, and sextants.

The entire space is covered in gears, cogs, and clockwork motifs. Even though I do not understand their mechanisms, a sense of assurance washes over me as if these instruments are working in harmony to guide the ship through the skies.

"If this tickles your fancy," the blob is back at the console, pulling a lever, "prepare for a true spectacle."

The ship shoots upward like a space rocket! I clutch the helm for support. Among the relics I saw before, there are large glass pressure gauges. The red needles across their dials are going ballistic. Through the gaps in the metal plates beneath my feet, I find the engine working harder than before.

And then, the view at the window transforms as we weave through the stratosphere, mesosphere, thermosphere, and enchanting auroras.

I gape with disbelief at Mage. They are leaning on the console, saying 'You're welcome' with jiggling brows and nods.

We pass a faint speck in the distance (a hundred percent certain it was the International Space Station!) and crown from the exosphere into blackness.

"We are in space!" I almost scream.

"That's such a passive, insipid word. Space." Mage closes their eyes, stands on tiptoes, and spreads their cape like wings. "We're adrift in the heart of the cosmos."

"Alright!" My jaw tightens, and I try to unclench my teeth before I speak again. "Please tell me what's going on? Where am I?"

"It's très simple. I want to wander. However, I cannot do that on my own. Today's voyage is around the solar system. We need a captain."

"Why me?"

"Who else?" Mage says as if I am the only person in the world. "Besides, you need this more than anyone else right now."

"Cool. Okay," I think aloud without looking at them. "It's a dream."

"Shhh, Little Worrier. This is an adventure. There." They point behind the helm at an intricately carved wooden hourglass the size of a book. Instead of sand, it holds a mélange of prismatic, grainy particles. The top chamber is full, with a few granules in the bottom one. "The stardust is slipping away. If we are not back before the top chamber empties, you will be stuck in a void. Worse. Stuck with me. So, all aboard the *Narrative Arc*. Chooo chooo!" They actually pull the rope to a bell, the chimes of which fill the entire ship.

The problem with being a mentally over-stimulated science fiction writer is that, in a situation like this, your imagination becomes your biggest enemy. A rational person would dismiss this as a vivid dream, but my mind meanders down various paths. Is this an alternate reality? Did someone trap me in a virtual world? Did I die and enter an alien overlord's simulation?

"That's what we tackle head-on," Mage says as if reading my mind. They snap their fingers. A liquid distinct from water cascades from the ceiling for about three seconds, drenching both of us.

"What the heck!" I mutter, wiping my face.

That's enough! Who is this person? If this is my fantasy, what is an arrogant stranger doing in it?

I am thinking of ways to escape Mage when my soaked pajamas dry. My mind clears as if someone has wiped away all the unnecessary information from the whiteboard inside my head. Instead of anger, I experience profound clarity (it surely has something to do with that liquid).

Rather than walking away, I ask, "How can a ship that has steam coming out of its roof function in space?"

Mage shrugs and then replies, "Maybe it's a secret known only to the moon-walking kangaroos and power-twerking bunnies. Hey, why do you think kangaroos are super jacked?"

Wow.

I suppress my next questions, which are:

How are we breathing?

What is the ship's power source?

How can we travel through space without following a trajectory?

Why hasn't this killed us yet?

Instead, "Does this ship have other rooms?" I need privacy. Stat.

"We have quite the assortment. There's…hey, look!" Mage points at a space rock outside. "Is that an asteroid colony?"

It's tempting to investigate, but I resist.

"Please tell me about the rooms."

"Sure, there's the deck, a dining hall, captain's quarters, a library, a galley…"

"Tell me where the dining hall is," I say as I walk away from Mage. "No, the captain's quarters. Wait. The library first."

After hesitating a bit, Mage leaps from the bridge onto the deck. "Follow me."

I scamper behind their flowing cape, staring at its unbelievable embroidery. Sequins, beads, and mirrors shimmer on its fabric, creating a dazzling choreography on my face. The sonorous bells of payal[17] at Mage's ankles ring a symphony. It extracts a hypnotized smile out of me. As if I am a child again, sprinting through the corridors for another mischief.

---

[17] Indian anklets

With my shoeless, socked feet behind Mage's mirror boots, we jog along the gentle gusts of wind that sweep across the deck. My mind buzzes with questions:

How is there gravity?

Where does this wind come from in the vacuum of space?

Why hasn't this killed us yet?

As we reach the rear of the ship, I am met with the most breathtaking sight I will ever behold. Even more captivating than the one from the bridge.

Lying in front of me, in all its glory, is a magnificent library, its backdrop—the Earth from hundreds of miles above. Stretching behind it, teeming with millions of stars, is the Milky Way!

Floor-to-ceiling bookshelves graced with rich motifs pull me toward them. Infested with greed, I run my fingers over the collection of perfectly bound tomes, ancient scrolls, and brass-cased journals, each a treasure trove of knowledge and imagination.

Yet, it's not the books that take my breath away. It's the cozy reading nooks scattered throughout the library, each one snuggled between more books. From a corner, a cushioned bench and a low wooden table beckons me. As I sit there and ogle at the Milky Way through the towering window beside me. Nebulae swirl around its galactic center. Leaning on the railing, I take it all in, the grandeur of the universe, feeling as though I could stay cocooned here all day, feasting my eyes, reading, and writing, serenaded by the airship's gentle hum.

Now, the ship has drawn closer to Earth's moon. At least it's following an astronomically accurate path. Whatever this may be, it's my personal paradise, and I am determined to make the most of it. My first destination: a teapot shaped like a steam train on the side console.

"Uh-huh." I hear Mage, and then see them pendulating their finger like a metronome. And to think they'd disappear if I stop paying attention to them. "Didn't you see that hourglass?" they say. "Do you seek to be marooned on this ship forever?"

"Of course!"

"Really?" They place one foot after the other in a princely manner. "Think about it. Here, for all eternity, without the people you love and the life you have built on Earth. Stuck with me."

My firm resolve to stay put melts as Mage continues to describe everything I cherish on Earth. It's scary how they seem to know precisely what would make me return to reality. With shoulders slumped, I follow them back to the bridge.

Experiencing emotions in their extremes has never been an issue for me. It's when two opposite emotions wed and choose me as their honeymoon destination that I lose my sense of self. The joy and interest sparked by this ship mixed with the vexation that steams from dealing with a stranger like Mage is nothing short of a torturous mental see-saw.

When I reach at the helm, I spot an ornate telescope. Next to it is a live map detailed with planets, moons, and some stars. The map is moving like a digital screen, but it's on a parchment! My resistance and skepticism give way to curiosity.

"What's that?" I point to a bird-shaped object in the middle of the live map. It looks like an asteroid, but I am certain it isn't one.

"That's a space monster, an Eagle heading our way. Shoot at it every half hour from that cannon." Mage points to a chamber beneath the helm. "It will weaken the bird and kill it before it reaches us. Remember, every thirty minutes!" Mage places a pocket watch in my palm. "That's when it appears in our range."

I've never been the person who frequently does something on the dot. Never even gone to bed at the same time straight for a week. The pocket watch, however, is gorgeous. It has a metal rim with a stunning gold cog embossed at its center. I press a button on the top, and the cover flips open to reveal the time.

As I am poring over the dial, I sneak a glance at Mage, knowing they're not looking at me.

If someone were to craft my polar opposite, both in appearance and conduct, they'd create Mage.

"Why can't you do it?" I ask Mage, detecting the scent of gunpowder on the clock.

"Because with great responsibility," they point at me, "comes great power. Now shoot!"

Mage is officially my outer space nemesis.

"Is that a living being?" I ask about the Eagle.

"Everything around us is living," Mage replies from a stool as they braid their hair in different styles.

"I mean, is it sentient?"

"No."

Relieved from the stress of another cognitive, maybe moral, dissonance, I squat on the floor and pull a liver. The cannon fires, hurtling toward the Eagle. I get up and peek through the telescope. Within seconds, my shot hits the target.

"Yes!" I hiss. "It's like a video game."

"It's not." Mage cracks their neck. "It's a task that you have to complete every half hour or we…"

"Yes, got it. What now? You mentioned the solar system."

"Let's doll you up first!" They rise from the stool, tapping the fingertips of both hands together, which prompted me to shield myself once more. "You don't have to embark on a space adventure in these dull-as-skull garments."

I glance at my creased gray and black pajamas, almost asking, 'Why not?' but years of people pleasing take over my answer.

"Fine. Let's see what kind of intergalactic couture you've got up your sleeves." I am just rolling with it now. If this is a dream, I'll wake up soon enough. If it's something else, it seems I have little free will here.

"Try me," replies Mage. "You want a skirt made of a river," they twirl, "and a top crafted from dreams? With a hat woven with clouds and shoes made of aspirations? Ooh, earrings made out of dark matter!"

How about curtains made of solitude?

"Give me denim shorts and a comfy T-shirt. For shoes…"

"The entire universe is your shopping aisle, and you're asking for the same stuff you wear every day? You are a writer, Feisty Chronicler. Use your imagination."

I do. I think of the most flamboyant attire I'd be willing to wear. Finding it hard to verbalize my vision, I ask, "Can you read my imagination?"

"Can I?"

To my wonder, I visualize an opening of a cave in my mind and let Mage pass through. Only to witness the image I hold, nothing more. That's the kind of power that empowers you when you are powerless.

Before I can banish Mage from my head, the magic happens.

My nightshirt morphs into an olive green corset, cinched at the waist to accentuate my body's frame. At its center rests a glass globe that seems to harbor galaxies within. Riveted gloves materialize around my palms, and bulky aviator goggles rest atop my eyes. I remove the goggles immediately.

The pocket watch, which was in my hand, now dangles from the neck by a chain alongside small, ornate keys. My legs bask in the warmth of well-fitted black pants embellished with brass buckles and straps.

On my head sits a hat ornamented with gears and vials of colorful liquids. I slide my goggles onto it and secure the hat in place. Lastly, a thick, utilitarian belt wraps around my waist, bearing a holster and a pocket, each housing a small telescope and a compact compass.

My body is crowded, yet it's comfortable and breezy as if I am still in pajamas.

"What about your hair?" Mage asks.

Voicing my imagination this time, "Make it longer. Forest green…" I blink and furrow, "styled like the aerial roots of a banyan tree."

"Now you are singing the Mage tune."

And with that, my hair lengthens and adopts a lush shade of green. Mage blows a gust of air, and they fly in voluminous waves. Can't deny it; it feels rather cinematic.

"What's aspiration-shoes?" I ask.

They plant one of their heels in front of them and swing it. "This!"

I observe my reflection in the mirrored shoes, grinning at the striking image, and watch as forest green kohl lines my eyes and a septum ring adorns my nose.

"No, not those. Surprise me." I also place my foot forward.

In an instant, the calf-high Stormtroopers socks vanish from beneath my pants, and knee-high brown boots in rivets and clockwork embellishment take their place. I notice that instead of stitches and laces, there are tiny streams of water flowing around the boots.

I mimic Mage's heel swing. "Bewitching."

"You're welcome." Mage clinks their shoe with mine as if we were toasting to my newfound style.

Shock had crippled me, but the fact that the new appearance is changing my mood stuns me. It's a belief I've always fought against—that my appearance could wield any power over how I feel about myself. I'm tempted to dig deeper into this newfound discovery, but I decide this is not the time and place for it.

Not going to lie. I look like a bard, a ranger, a rogue, and a wizard had an orgy and collectively conceived me to raise me in a spaceship.

"Try a kick," Mage interrupts.

Are they offering a weird drink?

"What?" I ask.

"Kick." They lift their leg and lightly hit the console.

With fisted arms, I lift my foot to kick toward Mage's waist. To my surprise, the foot flies up next to their neck. "Whoa!" I turn around and swing another kick, this time with the other foot, and it goes even higher, making me laugh.

"This is going on my resume," I mumble as I try a backkick. "Do you get hurt in this world?"

Mage swirls their finger towards the window. "This *is* your world."

I shake my head and throw another kick, this time toward the helm.

They take a protective cover over the wheel and scold, "Now, we have a trip to make. Let's hit the space road."

Mage explains to me the main console functions. To test the newfound knowledge, I reach the helm and gently swerve. The ship responds by turning. We glide past the moon, the steam engine chugging rhythmically. Outside the window, the lunar air fuses with the hissing steam, creating an atmosphere I've only seen in Japanese animation. Below, the cogs hum in a mechanical symphony, enhancing my unreal mood.

Mage shatters the reverie with a single sentence.

"First, we must make a detour and pick up a few passengers from Venus."

I make sure I heard that right.

"Passengers? You mean humans?"

"No, stegosaurus," they mock.

"There are humans living on Venus?"

Mage twists their mouth as if it's the most inane question.

"Why do we have to give them a ride?" A sudden weight presses on my shoulders and heats up my stomach. "I thought this was my adventure."

Mage grabs a chocolate truffle from a cabinet, unwraps it, and divides it into two. Opening their own mouth wide, they silently prompt me to do the same. I comply, blaming it, once again, on my need to not upset the opposite person. They deposit the piece into my mouth, and I relish the most velvety chocolate morsel I've ever tasted.

"What's the purpose of an adventure," they say, "if you can't share its splendor with other kindred spirits?"

That's disagreeable, but I don't argue, because my mouth is full with the delicious chocolate. Plus, the sand was trickling through the hourglass, and I didn't want to be stuck with the space dictator here.

We steer the engine toward Venus and land on its volcanic surface. The steam whistle roars. I force myself to stow away logic in the captain's quarters because, sure, there are people without space suits standing in the middle of volatile volcanoes, rifts, and mountains, breathing air that is over 95% carbon dioxide. It's impossible for humans to be alive here.

Knowing these probably aren't actual humans eases my anxiety a bit. Still, as I glance at the crowd through the window, they appear exactly like me. Real humans.

"Come on, Petite Comet," Mage says to me. "Let them in. Unlock the door to your heart."

Eww.

With little enthusiasm, I press a button, and a gangplank extends from the side of the ship. As expected, a breeze, breathable and non-lethal, sweeps through the deck. I try not to enjoy it even though it's warm and comforting.

Mage waves their hand to materialize plush antique chairs, a large oak table, and a refreshment corner stacked with food and drinks. Porthole windows appear on both sides, so do two glass observatories with telescopes and copper dome roofs.

"Welcome everyone! Let's take a stroll down the astral art gallery," Mage greets the crowd entering the ship—about a hundred people, mostly adults of mixed races, and a few teens. I survey the crowd to spot a familiar face. It might suggest the unreal event I'm experiencing is an intense dream. But every face I encounter is that of a stranger, each one radiating with excitement and curiosity.

Mage bends at the waist and whisper into my ears, "You get it? Astral art gallery? That's Mage for 'The Universe.' Whimsical, isn't it?"

With my arms wrapped around me, I glower at them and then at the crowd behind.

The passengers disperse across the deck. Some stand by the windows, gazing outside with awe, while others settle into comfortable seats with snacks in hand. A few peer through the observation deck with uncertainty, perhaps doubting if I am a proper captain.

"These people don't have their own ship," Mage says, pulling a banana from their vest and peeling its pink skin. "By taking them on this journey, you're providing an experience they wouldn't have otherwise."

Yet, here I am, the one who envies them. They could sit back and enjoy while I'm burdened with worries about piloting a ship, shooting space eagles, and monitoring hourglasses, all while dreading the possibility of being stuck in a void.

"So they'll be stuck with me in the void, too, if I don't complete this trip in time?" My question carries genuine curiosity but is marinated in bitterness. Mage's insistence on bringing others aboard has intensified my aversion to them. Few things irk me more than encroaching on people's privacy, especially when it's coerced.

"Wouldn't that be great?" They take a bite of the checkered banana. "Having them in the void instead of holding a one-sided conversation with your head forever?"

I blow air through my mouth and channel all the anger toward the ship's yoke. The ship rises from the surface of Venus.

"Smooth liftoff!" a passenger cheers from behind.

At this very moment, there is a utopian space at the ship's tail, yet it's forbidden to me. I imagine myself sitting alone in the library, feet up on the bench, inhaling the sweet scent of books while gazing into the heart of the Milky Way with a hot cup of tea, nursing me sip by sip.

"Cannon time!" Mage pokes my shoulder.

An uncontrollable urge to scream rushes over me. But the pocket watch indicates it is indeed time to fire at the Eagle. I squat and proceed, and like the first few times, the cannon strikes the target. Or whatever it may be.

As the ship sails through the ever-shifting cosmic currents, I contemplate how to free myself from the control of a stranger on a vessel full of unfamiliar faces. Escaping an outer space trip was never something I imagined in my wildest dreams. I would have given an arm for it.

Okay, maybe not, but you get the gist.

I shut my eyes in a foolish attempt to switch the difficulty level, just in case this was some video game.

Nothing changes.

We soar past Earth and its moon and adjust our course to head toward Mars. Through the side window, I catch sight of the distant, radiant sun—a tiny yet magnificent light bulb. Almost godlike. It entices me as if it's calling my name.

I steer the helm to change the direction toward it.

"Nah-uh." Mage steers the wheel back toward Mars. "It seems close. It is, however, millions of miles away."

Mage, the Sage, everyone.

"You'll burn yourself," they add, "yet never get there."

"Listen." I try to stay calm yet honest. "Firstly, this isn't reality. Second, you can't give me orders. I am not your slave, and—"

"You have the power to voice what's truly on your mind," Mage interrupts. "Come on, you've got this, Solar Flare Friend."

Why is it so hard to tell someone off?

Exhaling, I continue, desperation instead of firmness evident in my words. "It makes no sense why I must do this. This is a once-in-a-lifetime chance for me. You don't even know how many times I've fantasized about taking a similar expedition. If I wasn't a skeptic, I'd say this here is a literal manifestation of years of daydreaming. I really want to make the most of it. Do things I enjoy. Not this." I gesture toward the helm. "So, I'm going…"

"If what you desire," Mage interrupts me again, "is a once-in-a-lifetime opportunity, then so is this," they say, holding the helm. "At least you can imagine your fantasy. This, what you are doing right now, is beyond your imagination. Don't you want to experience something that you are incapable of envisioning?

Darn it.

Mage the Sage is right. Discovering the unknown and unimagined has its own high.

"Fine," I say. "But I can't commit to this journey without understanding it. Scientifically, it doesn't make sense. We should be dead by…"

Mage snaps their fingers and conjures the shower.

"You've got to stop doing that!" I try to snarl but end up grumbling.

Yet again, my clothes dry and the mind clears, as if I've awakened from a refreshing nap. I erect my posture and gaze outside with renewed determination as if I finally have a grasp on our journey.

After crossing Phobos, one of Mars's two moons, we hover over the fourth planet in the solar system. So many stories about it and its imagined inhabitants. Mars's oxidized, tan surface and red, iron-rich dust in its atmosphere make the planet look like…

"A painful space acne," Mage says, peeking at the planet.

The writer in me appreciates the simile, but I don't let it show and instead think about how far I've come from Earth. There is a narration running in my head, describing this escapade to others once I return to reality. Despite how it's happening, this is one of the best experiences of my life.

"Oh, here comes the parhttyyyy-pooper," Mage sings.

I hear clicking sounds before the pooper appears.

"Is that—" I stop mid-sentence. For some reason, saying the word "automaton" in front of an automaton feels like using a slur.

"Correct." Mage shakes their head. "The harbinger of all things dud and boring. That's Boink."

The automaton stands about a foot shorter than me, with a detailed, angular brass body dressed in a polished waistcoat and a tiny, metallic bowtie. It makes the sound of winding clocks every time it moves. Boink is a weird name for an automaton that has a Victorian monocle dangling from one of its glass eyes.

The automaton carries a tray of food to Mage, who, in the guise of taking something, places an object on the tray, chuckling. Boink then approaches me with the same calculated steps.

It has so many mechanical intricacies in its body, yet it exudes a human-like presence. I observe its crisp, plain, wrinkle-free pants, a stark contrast to the fabrics on Mage and me. The vials on my hat and belt are already in disarray.

"Stop staring at the automaton," Mage chides. "It's considered rude."

"Sorry." From the tray, brimming with an assortment of snacks, I grab a scrumptious-looking, hourglass-shaped samosa. The item that Mage had placed on the tray was a small tin of 'Machine Oil Lubricant.' Stifling a giggle, I thank Boink.

"You are welcome," the automaton says and takes a position equidistant from Mage and me. "You will drink water every half hour," it recites. "Eat every two hours, stretch every three hours, and sleep every fifteen hours. You must shower once a day and brush your teeth twice."

"The perky thrill of clockwork existence," Mage interjects.

This time, I chuckle.

"I and the captain," they continue, "can hardly contain excitement for the impending stretch breaks, Boink."

I offer a stoic nod, joining in on the jesting, hoping the automaton won't take offense.

And there, my brief moment of levity fleets away. A somber pall settles over the ship as if a melancholic plague is descending upon us. It's that same feeling I get when I have to attend a funeral.

"What's going on?" I ask, assuming Mage is experiencing the same dread.

"Dear self-professed space nerd, don't you know what awaits us after Mars?"

A small asteroid swooshes past our ship.

I feel cheated.

You can't be killed by something you've written poems and books about.

The next few asteroids race by at astronomical speeds—literally. Within minutes, we are officially inside what I had romanticized for years.

The asteroid belt!

A realization washes over me. It replaces the apocalyptic dread churning in my core with comforting assurance. I take a satisfying breath.

This is a perfect chance to determine whether this journey is a cheap trick or something closer to reality. You see, sci-fi movies, novels, and even illustrations in school textbooks have often misrepresented the asteroid belt. They depict it as a densely packed swarm of colliding rocks, hurtling at warp speed. In pulp science fiction, these asteroids typically pose a threat to the main character, who skillfully maneuvers their spaceship through this jungle, often deploying lasers to obliterate the said asteroids.

That is not accurate.

While the asteroid belt comprises millions of asteroids, they are widely spaced apart, making such dramatic encounters extremely unlikely without precise navigation. After all, the belt spans a region about 140 million miles across, with distances between each asteroid occasionally exceeding 600,000 miles!

So, if Mage intends to scare me with a theatric version of the asteroid belt, they can try. It'll prove that this whole thing is not just fake but a facade created by someone even more ignorant than me.

I consider Mage, waiting for their next move. However, they are already scrutinizing me, trying to penetrate my thoughts. Not happening. I lock the doors to my mind as tightly as possible.

"Trouble's on the horizon," they announce. "Brace yourself."

A sly grin curves my lips. Out with it, Mage the Sage.

"Not for the asteroids, as one might assume." They point toward a distant point.

I squint, frustrated that they didn't fall prey to my litmus test.

"What is it?" I ask. All I spot is a stony freckle. A meteor?

I grab the telescope and peek through it. A rock is hurtling toward us in my direct line of sight. Then another, followed by a third and a fourth. Soon, dozens more join the parade.

Something is off. They aren't moving in the typical meteoric orbits. My stomach curdles as I observe the rocks.

They have wings around them.

Windows.

And faces moving inside those windows!

"These are not meteors," I say in a shaky voice. "They are spaceships."

"You pronounced pirate ships incorrectly." Mage gloats.

I turn away from the telescope, fearing for my life. This might not be real, but that knowledge does not relieve me from experiencing raw human fear. The pirates are not aliens. They are like me, and humans are the most hazardous. Perhaps it's some evolutionary response. In this eighteenth-century ship traversing the vast solar system, the only thing that managed to invoke primal fear in me was humans.

I panic and read the same fear on Mage's face. For the first time since I met them, they stand in an alert posture, their cape hanging like limp hair, instead of soaring. They scurry around the control hub, searching for something. It shatters my assumption that I am in a safe space. Even if this might not be real, harm is possible.

Mage knocks on the copper tubes that run along the walls of the airship. These tubes seem to serve as a means of communication between people both inside and outside the ship.

"Check the parchment," they instruct me.

I obey to find various spots on the live map flickering, indicating the presence of pirate ships in the vicinity. A button labeled 'Accept' blinks on the side.

"Accept it," Mage urges.

"What if—"

"Do it!" they order me. However, the way they clench their teeth seems less authoritative and more like a younger sibling's tantrum, fearful of getting in trouble with the parents.

"You've got this!" Encouragement comes from a passenger behind me. I turn around but can't discern who said it. They all seem like one big bundle of fear.

Outside the bridge's window, the pirate ships loom larger and closer now. Taking a deep breath, I press the 'Accept' button.

"Intruders incoming," a pirate grunts on the radio.

"Are they announcing their own intrusion or calling us the intruders?" I ask Mage. They shrug, the former fear on their face now absent. I might have taken Mage's devil-may-care attitude as a sign that this isn't real, but they strike me as someone who would remain carefree even with their neck on a guillotine. How liberating it must be to waltz through existence unburdened by relentless anxiety.

I scratch around my arms and fidget with my tight corset before speaking into the mic.

"What do you want?"

"Make way out of this belt, nowish!" comes the reply.

They don't sound intimidating at all, which terrifies me more. It means someone isn't just orchestrating this as a prank.

"We come in peace." I can't believe I said that. For years, I fantasized about using that sentence. Now, it feels rather unsatisfying. "We are just passing through," I add, earning a nod of approval from Mage. "Let us leave."

"Bring forth yer captain," the pirate demands.

So, I turn the mic toward Mage. I've never wanted to be leader. To tell someone what to do had always felt totalitarian to me. It's why I never found out if leading is something I'm not cut out for or something I don't enjoy. There is no interest, however, in investigating that right now.

All I wanted was to sit in the library, quietly savoring the universe with a book in hand. But I am stuck here, challenging a bunch of space pirates.

"They should write books about you," Mage mumbles next to me. "Genre: The Reluctant Odyssey of Passive Seekers."

Shame slaps me.

I craft narratives where the first thing I do is place the hero in an uncomfortable world or situation. It's what helps propel the story forward and gives the protagonist a chance to grow. Yet here, my resistance to abandon solace clings like a shadow. In the vast expanse of space, surrounded by stars and planets, I'm still reluctant to leave my comfort zone, just as I didn't want to leave my desk at home to find inspiration outside.

Not acceptable.

Straitening my belt, I grip the helm of *Narrative Arc*, my knuckles popping veins. I retrieve the mic and declare, "I am the captain."

"Ye've set foot on your deck for a mere two minutes," the pirate sneers, "and ye fancy sailin' through our territory? Shoo…head back to yer Earth." They continue advancing toward us.

I think of the passengers, people who trusted me. What if I disappoint them? Get them killed? Get them captured? It's the kind of failure I can't bear, not even in a fake world.

"Have you tried rubbing your arms together?" Mage asks, stroking their inner wrists with each other. "It smells like," they take a whiff, "burnt matches!"

My pulse quickens. I am in this alone.

Drawing strength from my anger toward Mage, I grip the wheel. No, not to fight, but to reverse the airship. Of course, I can't fight them. I am just a fearful little nerd.

"Do you know what you have to do to get through the pirates? Theoretically?" Mage asks.

"Deploy the shields," I respond. "They'll push the pirates out of our path. Then accelerate before the shields collapse."

How do I know this? There is a lever in the control hub that reads, 'Shields to clear pathways.'

"Then what are you waiting for? A neutron star collision?"

Teeth appear from the tight line on my mouth.

"What if they get through?" I ask.

"What if they don't?"

"Fire the shields. Fire the shields." Half a dozen people chant from behind. Mage walks to the edge of the bridge and pumps their hands to spur the crowd. Even Boink joins in.

The fearful nerd in me is still ensnaring in doubt when the ceiling shower soaks me again. This time, I nod at Mage, thanking them for it.

With my hair still wet, I locate the lever bearing a medieval shield emblem. Another glance at Mage, and then I yank it. A translucent tunnel materializes before the ship, resembling the beam of a flashlight. It redirects the approaching pirate ships, pushing them aside. I throttle up, propelling the ship forward.

Though there's no wind, my forest-green hair billows, drying in the airflow. I feel like a badass. It's when Eye of the Tiger blares from the ship's speakers. I want to snort at the ridiculousness of it. However, the song pumps me full of adrenaline. Outside, the pirates stare at us from their vessels on both sides. I observe them one after the other, matching the sick beats of the music.

As we progress, their ships get bigger. They're firing at us, but the tunnel walls are devouring their ammunition.

"A view to die for!" Mage marvels.

Maybe their wish will be granted because the tunnel collapses. The translucent walls that separated us from the pirate ships are melting away. I pull the handle again to activate another shield. It displays an error message: 'Shield chamber empty.'

"What the hell!" I snap at Mage.

"What?" they shrug, "Go frown at Boink."

Before I can respond, a deafening cannon blast rocks our ship. The force of the explosion sends both of us tumbling from our positions. The pirates are firing at us, and it's clear their ammunition isn't disintegrating anymore.

My heart throbs against my ribcage. Murmurs fill the background. I hear phrases. "What a waste" and "she can't."

It's one thing to find yourself under the roof of Imposter Syndrome, but hearing others echo those same doubts about you is what walls you in.

A direct command burst from my lips.

"Everyone, calm the fuck down. Mage, either respond to their firing or get out of my way. I'll steer us clear of them. Boink, seal the breaches."

Unbelievable. Mage simply nods and takes their position by the blaster chamber. The automaton, with its clicking and whirring, descends from the bridge to raise a protective barrier around our ship, and the people do calm the fuck down.

"Trust me," says Mage, raising their chin as if they were balancing a ball on their nose. "This is where your real adventure begins." Their carefree comment grates against my nerves, but I digress.

The floorboards creak behind me as I clutch the wheel tightly. Cutting through the sooty smoke, a swarm of pirate ships converges on our position. I struggle to come up with the next move. Tempting images of the captain's quarters flit through my mind. The room has a bonsai tree by the windowsill and a delightful fireplace by the bedside. Maybe also a quiet corner where you can…

Nope.

I shake my head and guide the ship through an evasive maneuver. We narrowly avoid the relentless barrage from the pirates. I don't even take a moment to question how I know that. There is no time for reflection.

Mage plays their part, firing cannons and launching harpoons (harpoons, yes, you read that right). The first cannonball sails through space and strikes a large pirate ship, creating a brilliant burst of sparks and light.

"With warm regards," Mage signs off their cannon.

The passengers cheer.

Encouraged by their enthusiasm, I focus on my role and swerve the ship to the left to avoid an oncoming pirate vessel. Mage and I sway in sync to the left.

"Eagle!" Mage shouts.

I squat and fire a cannon toward the space monster. No time to check the telescope. The bottom chamber of the hourglass is already fuller than the upper one. I accelerate more, straining the engine beneath me. Steam billows like a volcano from the top, and the sails rustle with each gust of wind.

Mage continues to fire, hitting several ships and causing them to either disintegrate or change course. Most of the pirates' shots miss us, thanks to Boink's protective barrier, yet…

"Look out!" Mage warns.

I attempt to dodge but fail. A cannonball strikes the front of our ship. The floor rocks. Mage gets thrown off to a corner. I crash into the helm, and its wheel spokes stab my ribs.

Searing pain.

Fuck, this is real.

My skin burns from the impact as I struggle to return to the spot.

"We can…aoww." A groan escapes as I press at my abdomen. "We can take care of the damage later," I tell Mage. "Let's get out of here first."

Mage, who had fallen into the cavity between two consoles, raises their hand and moans, "Aye, Captain."

We navigate through space, dodging, weaving, and firing at the pirate ships. Our once disjointed efforts, Mage's and mine, become a synchronized dance of survival.

The ship coughs like an old man as we approach the last pirate vessel. Instead of evading or firing back, the pirate ship hovers in the void. I lean forward to inspect it. Their cockpit is empty!

"Where did they go?"

In response, Mage tilts their head toward the passengers. A heavy thud of footsteps lands on our deck from above.

It's the pirate!

Without missing a beat, I scream an announcement to the passengers. "Man overboard!"

Mage places their hand on my shoulder and says, "That's when someone from inside falls off the ship."

Shit.

Intrusive thoughts, one. Me, zero.

The plan is to retreat because my face is burning from embarrassment, but I find the pirate's lecherous stare, and it riles me up.

"I have a strong urge to lose my morals," Mage hears me say.

They give their blessing, "Treat yourself."

I vault the banister of the bridge and land on the deck to face the pirate. Our eyes lock, mine still teary from the jabbed ribs, his burning with predatory intelligence that overshadows his scars and tattered space suit.

We sprint toward each other, my solid boots thumping the deck. I unleash what I imagine will be the most valiant kick of my life. Just before my foot connects with his face, he counters by grabbing my leg and slamming me onto the unforgiving wooden floor.

Humiliation and pain surge through me as I lift my bruised face off the deck. My once-awesome green hair now a witch's fantasy. The eyes of every passenger are fixed on me, and although I can't see Mage, they sure must be enjoying the spectacle.

With gritted teeth, I push myself back to my feet. This time, instead of kicking, I launch myself at the pirate. My fist flies into his scruffy beard, and my knuckles meet his jaw. "Hah!"

He retaliates with a punch of his own, but I dodge with a grace I didn't know I possessed. In that moment, another sudden urge grips me—to live all over-the-top Indian action movies. I punch the pirate in his stomach and play the intense tempos of Bollywood fight scenes in my head. As if in response, the ship blasts "Duel of the Fates" from *The Phantom Menace* through its speakers.

I desired the drama of Indian score, not *Star Wars*, but again, I digress.

The pirate straightens and approaches me. I pivot, executing a swift kick to his chest. The music swells with the polyphonic sounds of the track and garbled Sanskrit chants from the choir.

Engaged in an epic showdown, I unleash a flurry of punches and kicks, forcing the pirate away from the passengers and toward the ship's railing.

"Boink," I call, summoning the automaton.

With precision, it raises the ship's screen. I throw one ultimate kick, landing it squarely in the pirate's belly. He hurtles backward and vanishes into the horrifying depths of space.

Cheers from the passengers create a chorus with one steady chant of Mage from the bridge.

"Asteroids! Asteroids!" they are pointing at the cockpit window.

I run toward the bridge, muttering, "One space problem at a time," and then ask Mage if they saw the fight when I reach them.

"You turning the pirate into space confetti?" they say, "Of course, I saw. Space brawls are the highlight of my day."

At first, it sounded like a mockery, but I recognized sincerity on their face. Blood rushed to my bruised cheeks, this time from flattery.

"Shoot." I glance at the live map. "Lots of incoming rocks."

"Yes, the belt might not be crowded. However, there are…"

"Swarms of space debris."

"Look at that big one." Mage points at a supermassive asteroid in the far distance.

My jaw drops.

"That's not a big one," I whisper, staring at a perfectly round celestial body, very much like our moon. "That's Ceres!"

We're about to take on Ceres. A freakin' dwarf planet hurtling through space at over eleven miles per second! From what I recall, it accounts for about a third of the asteroid belt's mass. There is no way we can blast through it or nimbly maneuver around it.

"Hey, look," I point at the brilliant, shiny object that distracts me again. "The sun. It's beautiful. Let's…"

"No!" Mage holds me by the chin and redirects my gaze. "Ceres. We bang-bang on Ceres, or Ceres bang-bangs us."

"Right."

"Here." They reveal a chamber.

"No way!" I want to be mad at Mage for not mentioning the laser blasters during our fight with the pirates, but a laugh leaks out instead.

Oh, what the hell. Here is to living another one of sci-fi's cheesiest clichés.

I blast one space rock after another, maneuvering around the larger ones. Our bodies oscillate in sync. The battered ship coughs up heavy steam again, trying to keep up with our shenanigans.

Ceres now looms dangerously close. Adjusting the blaster, I aim the laser at its rocky, salty crust and let it rip. Fragments explode from its outline and join the myriad of smaller space debris in the belt. Maybe one day, some of those shards will enter Earth's atmosphere, granting someone the chance to gaze skyward, close their eyes, and make a wish.

Tell me that's not playing God.

The dwarf planet, which moments ago occupied the view from our ship's front, is now shifting to the left. I keep steering *Narrative Arc* away from it. Without much thought, I glance at my pocket watch, squat, and fire the cannon toward the Eagle. This also gives me a glimpse of the hourglass. There are barely a few tablespoons of stardust remaining in the upper chamber.

Good news is, we arrive at Ceres with a substantial gap between us. Mage celebrates by dropping onto a beanbag chair I didn't know we had. As our ship drifts past the colossal stone, I'm relieved that we didn't have to completely obliterate a renowned celestial body. Although, I've definitely altered its trajectory by adjusting its mass and position.

Navigating the outer asteroid belt has been a challenge. From Hygiea to Vesta to those active asteroids resembling comets with their graceful tails to the Kirkwood gaps, it has been a brutal maze. You think of outer space as a calm, meditative place, but even on its own, space is violent, man.

So violent.

After Ceres, it becomes easier. I can now determine whether to veer or blast simply by assessing the size, speed, and trajectory of each space rock.

Sailing with this confidence, we reach the belt's edge. Right when I assume we are done, one more asteroid comes into view. An overwhelming feeling gnaws at me, akin to the days on which I publish my work or start rebuilding myself.

You are doomed to fail, is what that feeling says.

This last asteroid is not in our way, yet I swerve the blaster and fire at it just because I can.

"Some mercy, Celestial Slayer," Mage remarks from the beanbag.

The asteroid explodes into thousands of fragments, scattering like shattered remains of my fear.

Nah, fears. Plural.

The path clears, and our ship emerges from the belt to enter the sweet space of the outer solar system. I stand breathless, my chest heaving from the rush of adrenaline. I savor the exhaustion in my body and the soreness in my muscles. The massive emotions intimidate me, so I take a big swig of water from an antique glass Boink left me. It quiets the emotional flood a bit.

We had sailed for quite a while after the belt—I, quiet with my thoughts, and Mage, performing some optical illusions for the passengers—when I break the silence with a shriek.

"No…" is all that escapes my lips. Mage approaches me and follows my gaze.

Almost every inch of the bridge window is dominated by the surreal, cloudy landscape of what I've always considered my favorite planet in the solar system—Jupiter. Awe washes over me as I take in the majestic spectacle. The whirling marbled surface, painted in various shades of cream, orange, and pale brown, is thriving with powerful jet streams and ever-churning violent storms.

Oh, you have to be here.

With palms flat on the glass, I stare into the Great Red Spot, a spiraling maelstrom of crimson and ochre. A tempestuous eye larger than Earth itself within the immense canvas of Jupiter's cloudscape. I can't tear away from it, almost forgetting to breathe.

A storming calmness takes over me, even though it's the scariest visual I have ever seen. It's so hard to believe what's swirling in there, in that super-violent storm, is also swirling inside my body.

Why am I, then, not as strong?

My eyes fill up. I experience an unfamiliar connection with the universe, a sensation different from anything I've felt on Earth while reading about the same universe. I am not spiritual, but maybe this is what spirituality is. The knowledge that what binds the universe also binds me, and it's this connection that binds me with the rest of existence.

Mage sees me wiping my cheek. They direct my attention upward, pointing to the top of the window.

I tilt my head to spot a tiny testament to humanity's presence. Juno, the spacecraft, orbits Jupiter like an attention-seeking toddler circling their mother. To find a human handprint so far from Earth stuns me. I am not sure if that increased or diminished my respect for humanity.

For several minutes, I stand by the window, lost in thoughts. An abrupt, aggressive jolt reminds me that the ship is wounded.

"Ship down! Medic!" Mage yells, but no one responds. They frown with defeat. "Boink!"

The automaton arrives and gets an earful for not tending to Mage's whims. Then, it starts preparing repair supplies.

"Hungry?" Mage asks me.

My stomach gurgles at the mere sound of that question.

"Famished," I say.

They rub their palms against each other. "Let's go."

"Go where?"

"To where voyagers eat."

Mage takes the helm and lands the ship on a smooth celestial body. Most likely one of Jupiter's many moons. Icy crust, rigid surface with unrelenting hardness and no visible mountains.

"Europa?" I picture a stony moon in my head with dark, crisscrossing lines all across its surface.

Mage applauds, raising their thin eyebrows. In response, I throw in a non-humble smirk.

As we prepare to disembark, I freeze by the ship's hatch. Europa has plenty of oxygen. However, the atmosphere is too thin for humans to breathe.

"You'll live, Jupiter Gazer," says Mage.

Of course, I will. There were humans camping on the surface of Venus before.

I step down and take it all in. Breathing, as I expected, is easy. Better than on Earth. Although there is an uncomfortable tug against the expansion of my lungs. My steps fall one after the other on an unbroken sheet of ice that seemed to stretch endlessly toward Jupiter. The gas giant is sitting at the horizon like a huge, half-scooped ice cream. Even its faint rings are visible to my naked eye. It is eerie and captivating all at once.

"Have a seat," Mage says, setting up a couple of chairs they brought from the ship. The chair's arms have sleeves full of nuts, candies, and crackers.

I sit down with reluctance. Many scientists are sure that beneath this icy exterior of Europa is a saltwater ocean holding double the amount of total water in Earth's oceans. It's a horrifying piece of information to hold while sitting on Europa. My hunger dissipates. I imagine the ice beneath cracking and plunging me into the bone-crushing cold water or the jaws of an extraterrestrial sea monster.

I shiver.

To my relief, Mage distracts me by doing something unexpected.

Before the hoard of passengers who are disembarking to explore Europa, Mage is shaving water ice with a tiny chipper. Soft snow falls into their hand. They fluff the snow in their palms, shape it into a ball, and stick a pencil inside it. Then, they retrieve colorful bottles, one after another, from their vest pocket and drizzle the syrups on the snowball.

"Your favorite." Mage hands me their creation. I hold it by the pencil and admire the orange, yellow, and green hues on the snow. It's incredible how food impacts you. You could be sitting on the sixth largest moon of the largest planet in the solar system, millions of miles away from Earth, but a familiar treat can instantly place you back at home.

"Are you sure I can eat this?"

"Yes. Sanitized my hands and everything," answers Mage.

I laugh. "Thanks."

My eyes twinkle as I savor the tart green raw mango syrup on the Ice Gola[18]. Then I take a big bite of the fluffy, yellow snow and taste pineapple.

---

[18] A popular form of shaved ice served on a stick with flavored syrups

"You know," I say to Mage as they prepare another snowball for themself. "Growing up, we had Gola vendors visit our neighborhood every afternoon. We'd run to him with coins in our sweaty palms. If the vendor was nice, he'd drizzle the third flavor for free. You're a nice vendor."

"I can give you a rainbow of colors," Mage says. "Sadly, your palette is as limited as you."

It sounds like an insult, but they aren't insulting. I just know.

They take a seat in the chair next to me and bite into their Ice Gola. Their snow is dripping with gradients of colors, each sparkling like glitter.

"So," I finally ask Mage. "Tell me about yourself. How did you come to be…you?"

"Crowd, fear, town fair, Ferris wheel, marigolds, balloons, the moon, and there I was, born in the middle of all of it. You do the math," They answer, juggling three small rubber balls in one hand and eating a snowball from another.

"You expect me to understand that?"

"I must have existed before that. However, that's when I gained consciousness."

"Thanks for the clarification." I give up to move on to the next questions. "What are we doing here on Europa? What about the hourglass?"

"We are resting and mending," Mage answers. "So is the ship. Remem…" They drop the ball. "Drat!"

I release a deep sigh. This person has an attention span lower than a hummingbird at a nectar buffet.

So, I let my eyes wander too. Behind them, on the horizon, I notice Jupiter's Great Red Spot.

"Jupiter is my most favorite planet in the solar system," I say, not expecting a response.

"Because it's the largest planet?" Mage asks, placing the balls back into their vest.

"That's the thing. When it comes to Jupiter, people always think of its size. It is the largest, of course. But it's just a show. It's as if it has bloated itself to hide its small, fragile core."

Mage's childlike eyes reflect the shimmery purple of the snowball as they eat it and respond to me. "Jupiter is not sentient, silly."

"No, it's not, but when you read about its ever-evolving identity, you can't help but personify it."

"Ah, personification. Humanifying the abstract."

"A lot of scientists call Jupiter a failed star."

"Well, technically…"

"Yes, yes." I push my Ice Gola at Mage. Thanks to Europa, it never melts. "It's not correct, I know, and that's what I mean. It has no capability of turning into a star. Only because it's a giant, people assume it failed at having a greater mass. Or igniting nuclear fusion to become a star. Jupiter even fails at failing." I spit out a dry chuckle. "All of that is so…human. Jupiter is like that dorky kid who tries to bloat their chest and laugh a little louder so people know they exist. In reality, it's just failing and riddled with its own storms."

Mage has moved to my side, and we are both watching the gas giant, our faces bathed in Europa's hazy blue light.

"It's what I always picture when I see the planet on a screen back on Earth," I continue and point my chin toward the Great Red Spot. "Even that is its own doing. An anticyclonic storm. Jupiter spins so fast on its axis, it's created that violent storm within itself, large enough to gobble two to three Earths. Humans call it 'self-destructive behavior.'"

Mage retrieves a small wine bottle from their vest.

"Say what you want," they say, drizzling rosé on their snowball, "bloated, gassy, a failure or a cosmic misfit. Regardless, Jupiter's magnetic pull is powerful enough to draw countless wonders into its orbit."

It reminds me of dozens of moons, asteroids, and Trojans that revolve around Jupiter.

"I am sorry if I was rude." The words come out of me. I had been meaning to say that for a while. "This is not something I do every day."

"Prancing around the solar system?"

"No. I mean, yes, that too. But what I did back there," I glance at the ship. "Fighting the pirates and the asteroids. Just being there in the moment." Instead of mocking me, Mage is listening with kindness on their water-colored face. "I am usually in my head a lot."

"The bane of every writer's existence."

"But that's where the stories are made, aren't they? Why should I fight that?"

"It's what you do outside your head that inspires you to form stories inside it. If you stay confined in your mind, you're only crafting different facets of yourself."

I think about it for a minute.

It's the most groundbreaking discovery I've made in a while, the latter part of their statement.

"Maybe," I respond. "But it's not easy, stepping out of the head. It may come naturally to you. You are," I take in their persona, a bundle of marvel, "this. For me, detaching from my thoughts and living in the present is like…you know, I can't even start a book or a movie without constantly wondering about its ending throughout the story."

"The solution is very simple, Starry Companion. Stop being you and become the thing you are doing. Your mind is inside you; you are not inside it."

"That's not simple at all." I scoff. "It's as hard as asking…say, a seasoned surfer or a mountain climber to stay content only with the thoughts of waves and mountains."

The freshness that the Ice Gola had infused into my spirit fades once more.

"It's not a choice," I continue. "The world whirls by too fast for me to follow it. I am static in a world of perpetual motion. That's why I write. Within the stillness of words, I find my own ways to move."

"Thank the stars," Mage wriggles their fingers in the air. "Humans can do both: think of the waves and ride on them. You possess the ability to savor the journey from the comfort of a library, but you are also capable of firing cannons and fighting space pirates, accept it or not. Why, then, limit yourself to only one realm? You can exist in binary, silly. Go wild on the spectrum. Be all the shades. You discover yourself with a pen and paper every day; why not venture into uncharted spaces to explore yourself? Imagine missing out on," they stand and spread their cape around, "this!"

I don't respond and instead, retreat into the comfort of my head to ponder over Mage's words.

We finish our refreshments and watch Europa's first ever tourists get back on the ship.

"Do you know Abell 2146?" Mage asks.

I shake my head, still watching the passengers.

"It's a colossal system," they explain, "resulting from the collision of two different galaxy clusters, about two-point-eight billion light-years from Earth. Among the largest structures in the universe, containing hundreds of galaxies and vast amounts of dark matter. The collision in that system releases enormous amounts of energy. Surreal. Unlike anything witnessed since the big bang. That's Abell 2146." They look at me. "You can be Abell 2146. Allow the different clusters to collide."

A hesitant smile tugs at my snowball-stained lips, chipping away at some of the permanent hollowness in the chest.

Everyone, I can be Abell 2146.

"I think I know what's happening."

We are back on the ship. I had lifted off the grounds of Europa without Mage's guidance and sailed the ship all the way through the magnificent rings of Saturn.

"When I first came aboard the ship," I continue, "I wanted to be in the library. It was my comfort zone. You pulled me out of it to be here. Are you trying…is this some kind of moral video game?"

"Is this how you want to squander these precious moments? Analyzing?" They nod toward the window, where a distant nebula is unfolding a cosmic spectacle in slow motion.

"How much time do we have?" I ask. The hourglass had stopped making any sense to me. I am from the twenty-first century. I can't sense the passage of time by looking at sand.

"Enough to cross two more planets. We are about to reach Uranus."

I want to laugh, but it's the most overused space pun in the history of space puns, so I seal my lips. A moment later, however, Mage cracks up, and so do I.

"Seems like a tight entry," I joke.

We both giggle like goofy idiots.

After crossing Uranus, we reach the last planet in the solar system—Neptune. I titter at the absurdity. The planets of the solar system will never align because of their different orbital inclinations and periods. Yet we traveled in a linear path, crossing all the planets in a straight line.

"We are going to Pluto, right?" I ask with hope in my voice.

"Is it pre-2006?"

"It's also not the pre-1960s, yet you are forcing a woman to do things she doesn't want to."

Mage raises their palms in a mock karate stance and then retracts them. "Fine. You are the captain."

"Cool. To the solar system's reject!"

I land the ship in the heart of Pluto. Well, the part that looks like a heart, Tombaugh Regio.

This time, Mage escorts me to the ship's roof. We settle into reclining chairs, gazing up at the space. Time seems to stretch, as we simply exist.

"Actually," I break the silence. "My first favorite planet was Pluto. I come from a hot country. Since Pluto was the farthest planet from the sun, I assumed it would be like December and January—cozy and wintry. Then, I learned proper astronomy."

Mage offers a sweet, innocent smile that warms my heart.

Turning my gaze back to the sky, I continue, "Growing up, we'd have frequent power cuts during summers, scorching forty-degree-Celsius summers. Load shedding, they'd call it. It'd be so hot, we couldn't play or study or watch TV. So we would sit on warm-tiled floors, soaked in sweat, waiting for the power to return. When it did, and the fan blades took their first revolution, it would envelop us in this most blissful sensation. That's how I felt for a while here."

"Sorry for the incessant load shedding," Mage consoles.

I continue studying the ship's sail, which, by the way, is emblazoned with the emblem of a majestic fountain pen. Mage, on the other hand, is fixated on Charon, one of Pluto's five moons.

"Going on a walk," I say, getting up from the chair.

It wasn't an invitation, yet Mage follows me. We head toward a mountain peak, slicing through the gaseous forms of various ices—nitrogen, methane, carbon monoxide…what have you.

I lose grip over my emotions, having again fallen prey to the internal scuffle between what I am and what I should be. The incessant load shedding.

I look at Mage and ask them, "Do you know what happens when you put an overthinking, over-anxious individual in space without telling them what's going on?"

They don't respond, their face vacant for the first time since I've met them.

"Pure torture." Tears escape my control. "I am living the best experience of my life, and I don't know what it is. You ask me to live in the moment, but people can't just stop being who they are. I can't enjoy this if I don't know what it is. Where do I go from here? What happens next?"

Mage remains silent, urging me to finally ask something I've been too scared to ask. My biggest fear staring at me.

"Are we in my head?" I stop walking. "Am I losing my mind?" The thought terrifies me. Illnesses like dementia or Alzheimer's or schizophrenia, those that strip away your connection with your mind and steal your self-identity, have always been my greatest fear. It's why I don't consume alcohol. Losing control over my mind is too frightening. It is the only part of my body I trust. Then why is it leading me down this path? "Am I sick?" I ask again, "Hallucinating? Say something, please!"

Mage ignores my questions and offers his own, "Why do you despise me so much? I took you to places you've never been before—to the planets, the moons, and the asteroids. We are on a fantastical airship. I helped you fight the monsters and supported you. Yet you see me as some kind of burden. Why?"

I swallow the hefty lumps in my throat. "I don't despise you. You've been a great companion. But…"

"Go on." They fold their hands behind their back.

"You barge in as if you own me. Compel me to do things I don't want to. You…I am sorry, but you drain me. I also don't trust you. You don't seem…real. As if you are just my imagination."

It hits me like a meteorite. I freeze, the galaxies inside my corset's globe swirling like fruits in a blender.

Imagination.

Image.

Mage.

I stare at them. "Are you my…imagination?"

"Personification of imagination, Tiny Homo Sapiens," answers Mage. They twirl and take a bow, with their flashy cape blinking against Pluto's dark backdrop. One of their glass boots knocks over a rock, and they start to topple. I grab their arm to stop them from falling.

"Wild, relentless," I mumble, aboard my train of thought, "uncontrolled, draining. You *are* the personification of my imagination."

A spectacular explosion covers Pluto's sky, its thunder shaking us.

"Fuck! What's that?"

"Betelgeuse," Mage says. "It's dying."

I burst into laughter. Not because of anything else, but how lucky I was to witness that, in reality, or in imagination—watching a red supergiant star going supernova.

My hand reaches for Mage's, and we gaze upward. A magnanimous burst of energy and light.

Breathtaking.

Life changing.

I turn back toward them. "If you are my imagination, what's with all the other madness? The pirates, the asteroids," my arm touches the pocket watch on my neck, "the Eagle."

"That's everything you must confront to finish your last story. Or any story. To evolve as a writer, you'll need the same courage you displayed when you confronted those pirates. Be as brave as you were when you bested them. Have faith in yourself and your stories, as you had in your kicks."

I nod as tears cascade down my cheeks, clinging to my septum ring.

"The asteroids," Mage continues, "represent your fears. The fear of failure, criticism, not being enough, and the fear of losing your mind. Remember how you obliterated them? That's what you must do to navigate through that treacherous field of doubts."

Everything starts falling into place.

"You showered me with strange liquid every time I…"

"Overthunk," they say.

"Good made-up word…and the Eagle?"

"Your ultimate goal. Firing cannon at it was discipline and consistency. Learning to do something as small as pulling a lever consistently or writing for a few hours every day is more important than giving your all to it on one day and nothing for the rest of the week. Now you know you can build a habit."

"Wow." So much information in so little time. "The library." I remember. "It *is* my comfort zone. I was right."

"It is. The zone where you often seek refuge and resist venturing beyond."

A sharp light cuts through the luminescence of the supernova and blinds me. When I peek at the source, it entices me again.

"The sun," I say.

"Perfectionism. A formidable foe. Hey, solid alliteration!" They offer me their palm.

"Focus, Mage," I say, high five-ing them.

"The sun, perfectionism. You will never reach there. Even if you do, you'll only burn out in the relentless pursuit of it."

Mage is indeed the Sage.

I swing my head back, shaking it. This is insane, all the metaphors.

"Hey, what about Boink?"

"The everyday monotony. Waking up, exercising, showering, eating, taking care of yourself. The mundane yet essential aspects of life. As much as you'd like to call yourself one, you are not an alien. You are a human with biological needs."

I nod.

"Europa," says Mage, anticipating the next question, "That's just us indulging in a bit of whimsy." They cackle like a child. "Although you do need to rest and repair yourself to operate well. It's as crucial as putting in the work."

A wide smile spreads across my face. Intense affection for Mage wells up within me, knowing it's weird to experience that kind of emotion for my own imagination.

My gaze drops to the ground, landing on a stunning rock. I pick it up.

"What's this?" It's shaped like a meteorite and sparkles like the sun's gleam on an ocean. I peer through it to find it akin to a marble. On a closer look, I find kaleidoscopic patterns in it of all the places we encountered on this trip.

Mage is busy gaping at the supernova, so I pocket the rock and search for more.

Pluto is one of the most contrasting bodies in the solar system. There are even ice volcanoes on this little planet. But I wasn't aware of these shiny little stones littering its surface.

"Oh, don't act like a marauder," Mage speaks as I secretly pocket another stone. "You can keep them."

I grin and collect half a dozen rocks as we walk back to the ship. They feel heavy in my belt pocket, even though my own weight felt much lighter on the planet.

It isn't until we get on the deck that I remember the crowd.

"If you are my imagination," I scan the passengers, each one beaming at me, "who are they?"

"Why, your readers, Timid Mouse," Mage replies, tapping my temple.

Their answer untangles a knot in my stomach. "Of course they are." I smile and look back at them with gratitude.

"You carry them into your imaginative realms, and that's precisely why I nudged you to invite them in. With them by your side, your wanderings become adventures. Let them in with open arms. Some might not enjoy it." Mage singles out one passenger, who is snoring in a corner chair. It makes me giggle. "While some," they gesture toward a woman exploring every window with wide-eyed wonder, "might revel in your tales."

"What would I be without you?" I say to my imagination.

"Mind-numbingly boring."

"No disagreements there."

As I turn, Mage produces a rainbow-colored umbrella from their cape. They twirl it above my head and skip and dance along as they escort me to the bridge of the ship, occasionally opening and closing the umbrella to create small bursts of floral fireworks.

Laughing at their antics, I flick the flowers back at them.

"So, where now?" I ask when we reach the helm.

"To Earth."

"Ugh."

We lift off from Pluto. Mage pulls the throttle, and the ship swooshes into a vortex—a wiry, hazy tunnel.

After what seems like half a minute, the ship comes to a sudden stop. The vortex unvortexes, and I find *Narrative Arc* floating above Earth again. Not in space. Amid Earth's clouds.

"So, I most likely dozed off on my desk, right?" I ask.

"Existing solely within the bounds of your imagination does not diminish the validity of its occurrence."

"I hate those kinds of statements."

"I know, Interstellar Sprinkle." Mage guffaws. "Now, let's tap dance."

"What?"

"Follow my lead." They start stomping their boots on the wooden floor.

Oh, what the hell.

I mimic their movements.

"Remember," says Mage. "The best stories are buried within you. You need to live them to write them."

I nod and understand what's happening. The upper chamber of the hourglass is almost empty.

When I tap again, I notice the belt's weight. Retrieving the rocks I had collected from Pluto, I ask, "Wait. What are these?" A mild pain courses through my stomach. "Aaoow!"

"These are your ideas, silly. The untapped potential. Take them with you. Create something out of them."

I shove the rocks in my pajama pocket like a greedy kid. Oh yeah, the badass captain attire vaporized as soon as I retrieved the rocks from the belt.

"This is all so weird." I chuckle as I study the ship in my boring, dark brown hair. "It doesn't make any sense." The heels of my socked feet are digging into the bridge's floor.

"Not everything has to make sense," Mage responds. "Why else would I exist? For the nonsensical nonsense, of course."

"Sorry for despising you," I look above at Mage now, my knee deep in the floor. "Without you, I'd go nowhere."

They tip their hat and say, "Remember, you can…"

"I can be Abell 2146!"

My final glance in *Narrative Arc* lands on the last grain of sand falling onto the mound in the bottom chamber of the hourglass. Then, I drop back on my desk chair to the hammering sounds on the neighbor's wall.

I look around. No Mage. No ship. Just my home office.

Crowd, fear, town fair, Ferris wheel, marigolds, balloons, the moon, and there I was, born in the middle of all of it, Mage had said.

I must have been no older than six years, attending my hometown's Shravan[19] fair, my favorite. I don't recall with whom I shared the booth, but when we reached the pinnacle of the Ferris wheel, I remember peering below at the sprawling, constellated fairground filled with the clang, jingle of hundreds of people perusing stalls, waiting in lines, placing their bawling children on tiny elephants of merry-go-rounds, bursting pop-pop balloons with bang-bang rifles, tossing rings at soap bars, riding creaky rides, with their mouths open from screaming and laughing, and eating cotton candy and turmeric popcorn. People swirled around, some on teacups, others on motorbikes, around the perilous "well of death." On the other side, a crowd with marigold-loaded thalis cut through the oily, scrumptious scent of sago fritters to join the temple line.

---

[19] The fifth month of the Hindu calendar connected to the arrival of the south-west monsoons.

I sat in my booth, a static self, worried about passing through the perpetual motion to return home. If only there were another way.

Gazing skyward, with eyes fixated on the full moon, I envisioned my booth, just mine, detaching from the Ferris wheel and rising up like a hot-air balloon. It escorted me over the town, drifting above my school, the railway station, and eventually to the moon itself before gently lowering me back home.

There, on the Ferris wheel, under the silvery glow of the sky, surrounded by the vibrant busyness of life, I had met Mage for the very first time and escaped reality.

Mage is not in this room right now, yet they exist.

I close my eyes, take a breath, and reach for my pajama pocket to check if I still have the idea stones. A test to determine the level of my sanity.

As I reach into the pocket, a smile lights up my face. I hold the desk and pull my chair toward it. With ferocious fingers, I start typing the last story of "Take a Seat at the Cosmic Campfire."

Fragments of roasted puffed rice grind under the keyboard keys as I struggle to write the last story in my collection. Why do the final pages of your book have to devour your entire soul?

If you have stayed until here, please take a moment to leave a review on your site of choice.

It will help kickstart my biggest dream to be a full-time author.

AUTHOR'S NOTE

I hope the campfire was cozy and the stories toasty. As a farewell, let me share a bit about how the scavenging and kindling of the firewood came to be.

Over the years, I've read a multitude of renowned short sci-fi stories—from the enduring works of classic authors like Ursula K. Le Guin, H. G. Wells, Arthur C. Clarke, Ray Bradbury, and Isaac Asimov to the contemporary brilliance of Ted Chiang. But, as you dive into these popular names, you'll notice a little pattern—something I find absent in my own identity.

This realization prompted me to wonder how narratives within this genre might unfold with characters and perspectives seldom represented, especially when authored by someone not belonging to the familiar spectrum of these names. Moreover, there was a desire to entice non-sci-fi readers to explore this genre without intimidation, and thus, *Take a Seat at the Cosmic Campfire* (*TASATCC*) came into existence—a collection that blends classic science-fiction elements with my own literary touch.

Unearthing Idyll, my debut novel, served as a vessel for expressing years of suffocated thoughts, emotions, and ideas—it was a necessity. However, *TASATCC* is the work that made me fall in love with writing science fiction again. If my novel was a nourishing meal after a long bout of famine, this collection was the gourmet affair at Jules Verne's, perched atop the Eiffel Tower with panoramic views of the city unfolding below.

Each story in this collection was born from my obsession with multiple sci-fi ingredients, driven by a fascination with the mysteries of the universe and the profound moments of change that shape our existence. Through the lens of various sub-genres, I aimed to bring the unfamiliar to the familiar and traverse the depths of human (or non-human) emotions.

Whether you're a seasoned sci-fi enthusiast or a newcomer to the genre, I hope these tales ignited your imagination and pushed you to wonder about the vast unknown surrounding us. I trust it sparked enough interest in science fiction to encourage you to explore more. Writing these stories has been a journey of self-discovery, and I feel privileged to share my love for speculative fiction with you.

I extend my heartfelt gratitude to the readers of my previous book whose reviews and encouragement compelled me to finish another book this year.

As you turn the final pages, I invite you to carry the spirit of these tales with you—a reminder that change is the only constant, and the unknown is a mystical campfire on a cliff waiting to be explored. If you find some extra time, it would be super-cool of you to check out (if you haven't already) my debut novel, *Unearthing Idyll,* and support my dream to continue creating stories and writing more books.

In the solitude of your frigid forest, should you hear a beckoning once more, know that it's my voice, echoing from a cliff under a moonless sky so dark it mirrors the resplendent Milky Way. There, I'll be ready again with stories and beverages next to a roaring campfire, waiting for you to take a seat.

UNEARTHING IDYLL

BOOK ONE OF ASYMPTOTE UNIVERSE

CHAPTER 1

PacaSpace Transit Station
July 13, 2125

I am not lying!"

Lyra had raised her voice for the second time in her unremarkable life of twenty-seven years. It sounded like she spoke through a throat spiked with shards of glass.

"I had my documents with me just a while ago. There, at the café."

She rummaged again through her luggage, her sweaty tresses blinding her vision. In the last fifteen minutes, she had stubbed her toe, injured her shin, and bitten her inner cheek. This was not how she had imagined her first trip to Earth would be.

Lyra sucked in quick short breaths and pulled the neck of her sweater for some air. Despite the warmth, her body trembled. She would have blamed the centrifugal force of the rotating transit station, but the two delightful hours she once spent reading about the station's mechanics didn't allow her.

"Miss," an officer in a sharp, black uniform warned, "you are breaking Earthler laws by attempting to enter Earth's immigration without papers. You could be arrested for it."

A rotten taste swam up Lyra's throat as the soft buzzing of the station tingled her eardrums. She glanced at the travelers scattered around. Then she looked at herself—an ink blotch on a fresh sheet of paper. This was not how it was meant to go. She had dreamt of this day all her life. Her mind wasn't supposed to toss her the visuals of her comforting bedroom—the bedroom of the house inside an asteroid she had finally escaped.

The terrifying stare of the officer brought her back to the security line.

How is it even possible?—Lyra thought. How could her documents disappear? She had placed the folder back in her bag at the Spacebucks café...or had she?

REVIEWS OF
UNEARTHING IDYLL

★ ★ ★ ★ ★

From the very first page, Parekh's storytelling prowess shines brightly. The narrative is not only refreshing and insightful but also remarkably crisp, making it a perfect read. What sets "Unearthing Idyll" apart, however, is its profound exploration of philosophical themes. Parekh's writing style is nothing short of enchanting, and she has a remarkable ability to transport readers to the vividly imagined worlds within the book. The emotional complexity of the characters makes them feel real and relatable, eliciting a genuine emotional investment in their fates. A must-read for anyone seeking a thought-provoking and emotionally resonant tale.

★ ★ ★ ★ ★

An intellectual, emotional, wonderful treat.

★ ★ ★ ★ ★

It's unusual for a science fiction book to have characters that have so much depth and especially later on in the book, so much heart. I found the book really drew me in and moved me emotionally.

★ ★ ★ ★ ★

Not just for sci-fi fans! Great storyline, likable characters and a perfect pacing. Will be buying and gifting to friends for sure!

★ ★ ★ ★ ★

Dhara Parekh is a talented writer, and this book is a testament to her skill and creativity.

★ ★ ★ ★ ★

I usually am able to predict where the story is going, but the author took me for a ride! The author shows her skill in creating the psychological worlds of her characters, and in creating drama by making those worlds crash against each other. This is a story of self-discovery in the guise of a science fiction novel.

BUY IT HERE:
www.dharaparekh.com

FOLLOW HERE:
Instagram: @dha.raiter
Goodreads: www.goodreads.com/dharaiter

EMAIL HERE:
dha.raiter@dharaparekh.com